Penguin Crime Fiction
Editor: Julian Symons
Appleby's Other Story

Michael Innes is the pseudonym of J. I. M. Stewart,
who was a Student of Christ Church, Oxford, from
1949 until his retirement in 1973. He was born in
1906 and was educated at Edinburgh Academy and
Oriel College, Oxford. He was lecturer in English at
the University of Leeds from 1930 to 1935, and spent
the succeeding ten years as Jury Professor of English
in the University of Adelaide, South Australia.

He has published many novels and two volumes of
short stories under his own name, as well as a series of
detective stories and broadcast scripts under the
pseudonym of Michael Innes. His *Eight Modern
Writers* appeared in 1963 as the final volume of *The
Oxford History of English Literature*. Michael Innes
is married and has five children.

Michael Innes

Appleby's Other Story

Penguin Books

Penguin Books Ltd, Harmondsworth, Middlesex, England
Viking Penguin Inc., 40 West 23rd Street, New York, New York 10010, U.S.A.
Penguin Books Australia Ltd, Ringwood, Victoria, Australia
Penguin Books Canada Limited, 2801 John Street, Markham, Ontario, Canada L3R 1B4
Penguin Books (N.Z.) Ltd, 182–190 Wairau Road, Auckland 10, New Zealand

First published in Great Britain by Victor Gollancz 1974
First published in the United States of America, by Dodd, Mead & Company 1974
Published in Penguin Books 1978
Reprinted 1986

Made and printed in Great Britain by
Richard Clay (The Chaucer Press) Ltd, Bungay, Suffolk
Set in Linotype Times

1

'*Grove nods at grove*' – Sir John Appleby quoted – '*each alley has a brother –*'

'What's that, my dear fellow?' Colonel Pride, who had drawn up his car on the Palladian bridge for a preliminary view of Elvedon Court, glanced at his companion with every appearance of perplexity.

'*And half the platform just reflects the other.*'

'Ah, a bit of poetry.' Pride nodded. He was seemingly gratified at having got, as he would have expressed it, right on the ball. 'And I see what the chap means. All a bit formal, I agree. What another of those long-haired characters calls fearful symmetry.'

'Just that.' Appleby was never very sure about his neighbour Tommy Pride. The most antediluvian type of Chief Constable, with the Indian Army behind him, he was readily put down as one who would have nothing but Kipling, Sir Henry Newbolt, and *The Forsyte Saga* on his shelf. And he certainly played up to that image. But here he was, producing a neat little joke out of William Blake. 'Nothing that you could call forests of the night,' Appleby continued by way of appreciating it, 'but an uncommonly fine beech avenue. And not a clump of trees in the park that doesn't, in some subtle fashion, balance another one. You don't care, Tommy, for wild nature tamed and landscape-gardened?'

'If I owned Elvedon, I'd think no end of it. Tytherton certainly does. But one fancies what one was brought up to, wouldn't you say? My home was a Berkshire rectory, with a wild garden and a paddock and a hazel copse. What about you, John?'

'A back street in a midland town.'

'Well, that's dashed interesting, I must say.' Pride didn't know Appleby particularly well, and the Christian names were a matter of his having been a childhood friend of Appleby's wife. But he did know that Appleby had risen to be Commissioner of Metropolitan Police, and thus the commander of 18,680 men, which compared very respectably with the Guards Division. Like every policeman, he also knew that as an unassuming C.I.D. man Appleby had been a legend in his time. All this gave Pride honest pleasure in his recently acquired acquaintance, and he had rather taken to showing him off. It was precisely this that he was about now. But he seemed in no hurry to drive on. 'Much to be said for a middle station, eh?' he offered philosophically. 'I've never been much of a one for great houses myself. And I suppose Elvedon counts as that.'

'Well up the league table.' Appleby surveyed the mansion planted before them in the middle distance. 'Would it be by somebody chasing up late Wren, but with some older things in mind? It's like a larger Queen's House at Greenwich.'

'A bit in the same style inside, as a matter of fact. Symmetry and all that the thing there too. There's a big hall – rather a useless thing, to my mind – which is a double cube gone enormously lofty. And no end of small cubes making up the rest. Not really a graceful notion, would you say? Like living inside something made out of a child's box of bricks. If Maurice Tytherton shows you round, you may feel like wanting to pull the lid down by three or four feet. At least I do. Easier to heat that way – and easier for dusting too. But then I'm not a dab at architecture and all that, as I know you are.'

'Oh, I'll probably agree.' Although Appleby did in fact

enjoy gaping at splendid places it was his inclination to do so after paying his shillings at a turnstile and submerging himself in a crowd. He would be quite glad to get this courtesy call, as he considered it, performed and done with. 'I imagine our ancestors felt more secure in common-or-garden caves than in caverns measureless to man. Have there been Tythertons here for a long time?'

'Lord, no.' Pride seemed anxious to obviate misconception. 'Totally unheard of in the county three generations ago. And unrelated, so far as I know, to the great Whig family that built the place. Victorian bankers who won out when all the little local concerns began to be bundled together. Oceans of money now, but nothing immemorial about them.' Having thus perhaps reached an assurance that his friend would not be overawed, Pride appeared to judge it fair that something should be said on the other side. 'But a perfectly civilized chap, this Tytherton. Wykehamist – and father and grandfather at the same shop. Man of taste, too. Pictures and so forth. Lost a dollop of them, as a matter of fact, in a robbery some years ago. I expect he'll enjoy holding forth to you on that.'

'Most interesting.' Appleby was aware of a dark suspicion passing fleetingly through his mind. Art-thefts were known to have been rather his thing. 'What kind of robbery?' he asked.

'The case was closed a little before my coming on the job in these parts, so I'm not well up on it. Nothing spectacular, I believe. The thieves took alarm before getting at the best things. But the investigation, I'm sorry to say, appears to have been a flop so far as the police were concerned. I do know that Tytherton was very sensible about it all. Didn't raise all hell when our efforts were no go – as you must be so well aware some chaps do. Throw their weight about as people of influence, and all that.'

'Yes, indeed.' Appleby was decidedly not without memories of this kind. 'What sort of household does your friend Tytherton have?'

'So far as family goes, there's just his wife Alice – who is rather younger than he is, and a good deal livelier. Quite ready to make eyes at a fellow, if you ask me.' Colonel Pride paused. 'John,' he added hastily – thereby indicating that this is something one doesn't say about a woman except to an intimate friend. 'There's only one child, a grown-up son by a former marriage, called Mark. He must be the heir to a good deal. But he lives in Argentina, where he's said to look after various substantial family interests. Never seems, though, to hop on a jet and visit dad and step-mum.'

'And that occasions gossip?'

'Bound to, eh? There are people who claim to remember Mark Tytherton as a bad hat. Malicious twaddle, as likely as not. He may be a dud, of course, but that's not the same thing.'

'Not remotely.' Appleby had listened not without amusement to Colonel Pride's entirely gentlemanlike way of straying into scandal. 'Mark may merely be a mild drunk, or a little given to drugs, or not to be trusted with the housemaids.'

'Quite so. Anything of that kind. Then there's a nephew, also of the name of Tytherton, who comes and goes. Archie Tytherton. No notion what his line is, but it seems to allow him a good deal of leisure. That's the whole family, so far as I know. The only other regular is a fellow whose name I forget. No I don't. Ramsden. Something-or-other Ramsden. He's unmarried, and lives in the house, and seems to combine managing the farms and acting as Tytherton's personal secretary. Perhaps we'd better drive on.'

They ran over the bridge – a structure which could not quite escape the charge of having been built for ostentation, since it elaborately spanned a channel that need not have been there at all. The waters on either hand were very much of the ornamental order, achieved by a certain amount of excavation and the diverting of a stream. The scene, Appleby reflected, was a pious fraud, since it represented the entire reassuring spectacle – the sparkling lake, the variegated water-lilies, the even more variegated water-fowl, the pendent willow, the soaring pine, the pleasing alternations of boscage and grassy sward – as the regular habitat provided for man by a truly amiable deity: or as this after man himself had applied to it no more than the finger of taste.

So much for the prospect now on Appleby's left. On his right stood Elvedon Court, confidently aloof behind a spreading lawn, a low balustrade, a terrace surveyed by here a robed philosopher and here a naked nymph surprised. Elvedon couldn't, as did its park, pretend to be a mere emanation of great creating Nature, but it did reflect a just repose and confidence in a divinity of eminently mathematical mind, who never got his sums wrong. The place was like an elegant ledger, exactly balanced and therefore perfectly secure.

Esteeming proportion highly can, of course, have social consequences. The house was, for its kind, unusually lofty, so that from the lantern crowning it there must be a splendid view. Superimposed upon a heavily rusticated ground floor were two stories with an identical fenestration, and above this again was some region of lesser consequence beneath the leads. The effect might have been a shade topheavy had the answering basement level not been dug deep into the earth. Because God must be declared the Perfect Cube – Appleby told himself – you condemn your manservants and maidservants to a more or less troglodytic life.

'Peaceful,' Pride said. And he added, 'Coming this way,

we have to run round the house. The main entrance is on the north side.'

'Decidedly peaceful. Built by people who felt themselves to be ever so securely in the saddle. But who knows? A molehill or a rabbit hole – and over go horse and rider.'

'Very true, John.' Pride swung the wheels of the car. 'Or up jumps beside you the devil knows what, and the rest of your ride isn't to your liking. *Post equitem sedet altra Cura* – eh? Wonderful way of putting things, Horace had. Appeals even to a boy. Like to have another look at him one day. But Latin a bit rusty, I expect.'

'*Horace still charms with graceful negligence.*' Appleby was watching the west front of Elvedon go by; its mild severity was relieved by a recessed loggia the columns of which were flush with the main walls.

'So he does, to be sure.' Gratified by this classical turn which he had introduced into the conversation, Pride swung the wheel again, so that the main approach to the house was before them. 'Money and lands and palaces are no barrier to black Care, I agree. But no reason to suppose anything of the sort is stalking Elvedon Court at the moment.'

'Black Care?' Appleby had jerked back in his seat. 'Well, I don't know about that. But there's certainly what we used to call a Black Maria.'

This was true. Bang before the stately flight of steps leading to what, in a humbler dwelling, would be called the front door stood a sinister police van. Its rear windows, latticed in steel, were like the eyes of Justice, blind or indifferent to place or greatness. The doors in which they were set were prepared to open dispassionately, upon due occasion given, for the reception of gentle or simple, rich or poor. But this was not all. Two large police cars stood parked in front of this ominous receptacle. On the roof of one of them a circling electric beacon had been left on to no particular purpose. But it was plain that, for reasons unknown, the local constabulary had arrived in force.

'God bless my soul!' Colonel Pride, within whose jurisdiction the officers who must have turned on this exercise lay, seemed disposed to regard some official impropriety as having taken place. 'What the devil are they up to? And not one of the fellows in sight. Anybody could make off with those damned cars.'

'They must all be inside, grappling with a gang of desperadoes. Heartening for them, Tommy, to have their Chief Constable turn up so promptly to lend a hand.'

'Don't be absurd. There isn't a sound.'

'Perhaps they're all dead. The representatives of crime and of the law have eliminated each other to a man. Also Maurice Tytherton and all his quality.' Appleby had climbed from the car. 'It's more probable, however, that what has happened is entirely prosaic and unremarkable.'

'Well, that's a much more sensible remark.' Pride had joined Appleby before the steps of the mansion. 'Somebody had another go at Tytherton's confounded pictures – that's my bet.'

'And, after their former ill success, your people are mounting a really impressive operation. Tumbling over each other, Tommy, in their haste to obliterate anything that could be called a clue.' It was half seriously that Appleby spoke; he had never much gone in for spectacular parades. 'Perhaps we'd better go away. The circumstances don't seem propitious for a polite call.'

'My dear chap, whatever it is, I must obviously muck in.'

'Then I'll take a turn round the lake, and hope to see you emerge in about half an hour.'

'No, no – we must carry on together. Dash it all, John, it may be something absolutely up your street.'

11

'So much the worse. I haven't retired from the Yard, you know, to play Sherlock Holmes.'

'Perhaps not. But there was that affair –'

'There have been several affairs, I admit. But the general proposition holds.'

'Really, John, we're making too much of this.' It was with a considerable effect of cunning that Pride thus shifted ground. 'We'll just drop in, pay our respects to the Tythertons, and find out what these theatricals are about. Then we'll come away. Later on, I can return officially, if there seems any point in it.'

'Very well.' Appleby spoke with resignation. 'But just remember, please, that I'm not interested in stolen pictures. Repeat *not*.'

'Then that's agreed.' Pride had already begun to climb the flight of broad steps before them. 'And we'll start by behaving as if we'd noticed nothing out of the way.'

This last appeared to Appleby an implausible proposal. But Pride stuck to it. Pausing before an impressively massive door, he rang a bell, and waited. The door opened almost at once upon the figure of a sombre manservant.

'Is Mr Tytherton at home?' Pride asked formally.

'Yes and no, sir.'

'What's that?' Not unnaturally Pride was startled by so absurd a response from a well-trained butler.

'My Tytherton is in the house, sir, but unfortunately he is unable to receive visitors.' The butler paused, and it suddenly came to Appleby that he was conceiving himself as breaking something gently. This proved true. 'I regret to say that Mr Tytherton is the *late* Mr Tytherton. He was shot dead last night.'

2

One must look on the bright side, Appleby told himself as he stepped into the hall of Elvedon Court. He had been entertaining a notion – perhaps baseless, yet supported by a good deal of experience – that there had existed, as it were, wheels within the innocent wheels of Tommy Pride's car; that the morning's expedition had owned a basis in some desire expressed by the late Maurice Tytherton to confabulate with the country's acknowledged authority on art-robberies. The man hadn't really reconciled himself to the loss of whatever had been filched from him; he had heard of Appleby as a friend of Pride's; and he had taken it into his head that here was a chance of getting a fresh and better-directed hunt started. Some nonsense like that. However, Tytherton *was* now the late Tytherton – as his butler had with a kind of mournful satisfaction announced. Perhaps he would recover his missing pictures in heaven. It was said to be a well-ordered place; perhaps an efficient lost property bureau operated there.

If Appleby was conscious of disapproving of this profane fancy in himself, the reason was possibly that he had suddenly become aware of being in the presence of a clergyman. He had firmly sat down in an unobtrusive corner of the hall, and let Pride go about his inquiries on his own. The statistical probability was that the proprietor of Elvedon had made away with himself. It is a good deal more common to contrive *that*, or even to contrive a sheer imbecile accident

13

with a lethal weapon, than it is to get oneself murdered. Anyway, in whatever fashion Tytherton had died, Appleby felt not the slightest disposition to get involved in the matter. So down he had sat. And now here was a parson, showing some inclination to converse. Appleby stood up.

'Sir John Appleby?' the parson said.

'Yes. I came over with Colonel Pride to call on Mr Tytherton – a man I'd never met.'

'Ah, yes. May I introduce myself? My name is Voysey, and I am the vicar here.'

'How do you do.' As Appleby produced this civil formula (with the austerely non-interrogative inflexion which English convention decrees) he noted a look of sharp appraisal on the part of his reverend interlocutor. He was being sized up. The fact struck him as so odd that he made, as it were, a somewhat random grab at appropriate platitude. 'This,' Appleby ventured, 'is a very sad business.'

'For the bereaved persons – if there are genuinely any such – that is undoubtedly so. Of course it is my professional duty to adduce certain countervailing considerations. My dear Sir John, let us sit down.'

Appleby sat down. He sat down almost abruptly. This was because of a feeling – a positively sinister feeling, familiar to him from the past – that the elderly cleric interested him. He found himself trying to think up some inoffensive formula of disengagement. For he did *not* propose to let his mind so much as begin to operate on whatever commonplace thing – crime or mere fatality – had befallen at Elvedon Court. Perhaps, he thought, he could firmly start a conversation on the weather. But Mr Voysey prevented him.

'A sad business, no doubt. And apparently a bad one into the bargain. But that would not be my own first and spontaneous characterization of the affair.'

'Indeed?' It occurred to Appleby to wonder whether in

his pulpit Mr Voysey indulged himself in this manner of address. If so, he must impress rather than enlighten the more rustic part of his congregation. 'Then how do you view it?'

'As a pretty kettle of fish, my dear sir.' Mr Voysey appeared to enjoy his abrupt change to a colloquial note. 'And what will happen, I ask myself, when the police take the lid off? What, let us say, will be the resulting smell? A very fish-like smell, of course. Conceivably, a variety of ancient fish-like smells. And will they fix on the right one? I am a little worried about that. I could almost wish they should not prise the lid off at all. And perhaps they won't. It has not, of course, been my business to take much note of them, but circumspection strikes me as their chief anxiety.'

'I don't think I understand you.' Appleby had frowned. 'Do you mean that the police are dragging their feet?'

'Something of the sort was how I felt about them when there was an odd business of stolen or missing pictures a couple of years ago. Might one call them respecters of persons? I should judge the general air of this place to slow them down a little.'

'Colonel Pride will cut through anything of that sort.'

'It is to be hoped so. Or perhaps you will.'

'I have nothing whatever to do with the matter.' Appleby was looking at Mr Voysey in astonishment. 'I suppose you may have heard of me, and be imagining I am still on an active list. I am not. And, even if I were, such an affair as this wouldn't remotely come my way. My presence here is totally fortuitous.'

'Your reputation is known to me, I confess. But perhaps, Sir John, I am under a misapprehension as to why Colonel Pride and yourself have arrived together, hard upon this grim news.'

'I think you are. When we arrived at Elvedon just now,

neither Pride nor I had a notion of Tytherton's being dead. Haven't I made that clear to you already, Mr Voysey? Quite literally, we came to pay a call.'

'I see, I see. But at least Pride is now the responsible man. And if he does interest you in the mystery, after all –'

'The mystery?'

'I think it will certainly turn out to be that, Sir John. If he does interest you in it, I shall be relieved. I don't know that I greatly care for these people.' Voysey made a gesture as if to embrace Elvedon Court at large. 'But they are *in* my care, are they not? In a pastoral sense, that is.'

'No doubt.'

'And I would not like to see some miscarriage of justice befall.'

'You have positive reason to fear something of the kind?'

'It is like this, Sir John.' Voysey paused, as if to collect himself. If there was something mildly eccentric about him, he seemed nevertheless entirely serious. 'They are a curious crowd. Some of their relations would have to be described, I fear, as not wholly edifying.'

'The household here at Elvedon?'

'That – and some of their acquaintance. My fear is that the local police will simply seize upon whatever happens to be the first thing to turn up, and perhaps pursue it to the exclusion of so much as noticing others.'

'I think they can be relied upon to take a pretty comprehensive view. Police are famous, Mr Voysey, for leaving no avenues unexplored.'

'It may be so. But take, for instance, Mark.'

'I beg your pardon?'

'Mark Tytherton, the dead man's son, and his heir.'

'Who lives in Argentina, and never visits England?'

'Quite so. I perceive you have already been making inquiries.'

'Nothing of the kind, sir.' Appleby was annoyed. 'Pride has merely given me some account of the family as we drove over.'

'Ah, to be sure. But my point is the possibly prejudicial character of the coincidence of Maurice Tytherton's death with his son turning up at long last. For he *has* turned up. And that's not all. But perhaps, Sir John, you judge me importunate – that I am unwarrantably obtruding these matters upon you?'

'It would be uncommonly hard to say that you were not. But, having got so far, we'd better go on. Just where has Mark Tytherton turned up, and what do you mean by speaking of his return as "not all"?'

'I mean the clandestine character of the thing. A couple of days ago I simply came upon him in the park. My identification of him was most positive, but he was aware of me only as a passer-by. I have since made discreet inquiries, and know that he has not shown up at the house.'

'I see.' Appleby paused, and looked hard at the vicar. 'Well, that is information which you must give to the officers in charge of the present inquiry.'

'I am afraid you are right.' Voysey paused in his turn. 'If I didn't know it was my duty to tell *them*, it is improbable I should be telling *you*. And I hope I have made my general position clear.'

'What I think you are telling me is this: the situation here at Elvedon is such that any one of quite a variety of causes may lie behind its owner's violent death, and that they should all be investigated before any conclusion is arrived at. In particular, we shouldn't be too impressed by what sounds a very odd piece of behaviour on the part of his son. Would you describe yourself, sir, as having a liking for Mark Tytherton?'

'As you already know, neither I nor anyone else here has

an opportunity of forming an opinion of him over rather a long period of time. But, for what it is worth, I am afraid the answer is no.'

'I see. Is there, in fact, anybody here for whom you feel your sympathies enlisted?'

'Let me first give you, Sir John, what you may regard as the proper parsonical reply. I hope to feel a fully human sympathy for all with whom I am brought in contact. Apart from that ... well, let me put it another way. At Elvedon I have no axe to grind. But I am very glad that you have asked me a question. It augurs well.'

'I must really insist –'

'And I shall always do my best to answer any others. But now' – and the vicar gave Appleby a faintly ironic glance – 'I must be off about my true business of visiting the good poor. My vicarage, by the way, is no more than a couple of hundred yards off, beyond our late friend's kitchen gardens. Good morning to you.'

Appleby endeavoured to relax again. It was true, he reflected, that he had asked a question. In fact he had asked several questions. But there was no need to regard himself as having thus got on a slippery slope. The Reverend Mr Voysey, so oddly and insistently communicative, had taken him unawares and given his professional curiosity a nudge. There was no denying that. But it ought not to be really difficult to coax it to sleep again.

He got up and strolled round the hall, which rose to a domed roof with a lantern at a great height above. The floor was laid with black and white marble, and between engaged columns on the walls hung uninteresting portraits of prosperous persons by Herkomer and other fashionable painters of the later nineteenth century. These presumably represented the Tythertons making, as it were, an immediate and frank avowal of the period of their own rise to consequence. Nobody would want to walk off with square yards of that sort of canvas, so presumably the deceased Maurice Tytherton's major treasures (or what remained of them after the more or less recent robbery) were hung somewhere else in the house. There must certainly be plenty of room for them.

There wasn't a soul in evidence – except that Appleby could see that a police constable had now been stationed outside the front door. There wasn't even a murmur of talk. Silence is of course appropriate to a household in mourning, but from somewhere one might expect to hear at least voices briefly engaged, or an opening or shutting door. Nothing of the kind. Yet there must surely be a substantial number of people around. Servants, for example. The personage who had admitted Pride and himself to the mansion wasn't the sort who consents, even in the nineteen-seventies, to getting along without a sizeable squad of underlings. But there wasn't so much as the scurry of an apron. Whatever was going on, was going on at a remove from these central splendours amid which Appleby had islanded himself.

It was true that the household itself, as Pride had sketched it, wasn't a large one. There was the second Mrs Tytherton, now a widow, with whom Mr Voysey had presumably been closeted. There was perhaps a nephew – who was said to come and go. There was a secretary. Apart from the possibility of house guests – always to be reckoned with in a place running on this scale – that was it. Except, of course, for the enigmatically non-resident Mark.

Appleby paused, frowning, in front of a Lawrence. It represented a whiskered gentleman in broadcloth, who was pointing a quill pen at an open ledger in a manner reminiscent of a Field Marshal pointing with his baton at a map. Lawrence hadn't thought much of this commission, and had made a flashy job of it. The sitter was perhaps the original, the first mentionable, Tytherton. Appleby moved on. Perhaps Mark Tytherton, more or less lurking in a shrubbery, was to be, correspondingly, the last of the line.

A very odd yarn – that of Voysey's. The long-lost, bad-hat heir returns in secret to the neighbourhood of his ancestral home, and a horrid murder succeeds. When you were handed a melodramatic set-up like that, Appleby told himself, it was invariably rubbish. One could say of it, as in the curtain-line of Ibsen's play, that people don't do such things.

Not that they don't do other things which are a great deal odder. He had seen much that was bizarre in his time. But he hadn't seen much that was bizarre *lately* ... Quite conceivably, the sudden end of Maurice Tytherton might be at least not a simple affair. That had really been the burden of the Reverend Mr Voysey's discourse : that odd and intricate relationships were the order of the day at Elvedon Court, and that Tytherton's decease might well beckon an inquiring mind into them.

With a movement almost too abrupt to be either aesthetically decorous or physically safe when walking this marble sea, Appleby turned away from Sir Thomas Lawrence's negligent and condescending daub, and sought the open air. It had been a mistake to enter this confounded house with Tommy Pride; his presence was otiose, anomalous, and out of time. He was a comfortably retired man. He would withdraw to Elvedon's nearer policies, and be comfortably retired there. Tommy Pride could come and bellow for him – or set his cops hunting him – when it was time to go away.

The constable beneath the portico jerked to attention, and saluted Appleby with a rigidity that could not have been exceeded had the visitor been the Monarch and her Consort rolled into one. Word, in fact, had got round. The Chief Constable himself had arrived – and with him he had brought John Appleby.

Perhaps, Appleby thought, there was a maze or a grotto or an abandoned ice-house – some nook where (like Mark Tytherton of Argentina) he could lurk. If he got himself mixed up in the death of this wealthy and obscure merchant banker, his grandchildren would echo their parents' affectionate laughter. He was as much on the shelf as that.

He walked down the stately steps, consciously resisting the undignified scamper of a fugitive. The July day was gorgeous, but now uncommonly hot. He walked across a gravel sweep, through an archway in a high wall, and into a formal garden beyond which lay an expanse of woodland apparently traversed by winding paths. It would be pleasantly cool in there, he thought, and made his way to it. Within minutes Elvedon had vanished, hidden behind stately beech trees and agreeably random hazel thickets. So that was that. He would drop Maurice and Mark Tytherton, and think of something else.

He rounded a bend and found himself in a small glade. In the middle of it, on a fallen trunk, a man was sitting, seemingly lost in profound reflection. For a moment Appleby thought that this might be the mysterious Mark. Then he saw it couldn't be – simply because it was somebody he knew very well.

'Good morning,' Appleby said drily.

3

It would be theatrical to declare that, very suddenly, the die was cast. But Appleby certainly felt himself, as he eyed the man called Egon Raffaello, moving perceptibly nearer to the life and death of Maurice Tytherton. The uninteresting story of some theft or burglary which had resulted in the loss of a number of not-all-that important pictures: this had instantly turned, as it were, three-dimensional. A curtain with some conventional scene depicted on it – a stately home appropriately surrounded by gardens and park – had unexpectedly lifted. And what stood revealed was a solid set, handsomely stage-carpentered, which (to hold the metaphor) was irresistibly beckoning Sir John Appleby to step across the footlights and take up a familiar role.

'Oh, good morning,' Raffaello said. He had jumped to his feet and was still uncertainly poised on them – much as if not wholly without the thought of taking to his heels. But his voice was steady enough. 'How curious, my dear Commander, that we should meet at Elvedon. But I am forgetting. Not Commander. Sir John. I think, in fact, you run the whole show? I congratulate you.'

'Thank you. But I have retired. It's some time – is it not? – since we effectively met. Perhaps you will allow me to say that I have continued to follow your career as well as a secluded countryman can. A compulsive interest attaches to a charmed life, don't you think?' With the effect of one owning a good deal of leisure, Appleby sat down on the tree trunk from which Raffaello had started. 'Do you know that after the Nessfield affair I thought they had you? But not a bit of it. Here you are, never having had to listen to a judge's hard opinion of you in your life. So *I* congratulate *you*.'

'You can't be said to be turning civil, Appleby. I fear a morose and acrid dotage is ahead of you. What you have just been saying, by the way, if heard by witnesses, would probably be actionable. And I should be in quite a strong position to sue. No doubt I am regarded as what is called a keen business man. But no art dealer could stay in business without being that. The fact is, I am enormously respectable.'

'You are most assuredly nothing of the kind. In fact, no adequately informed person would much want to have dealings with you – except, perhaps, for purposes of an irregular sort. So I find your presence at Elvedon interesting. I take it you are staying in the house?'

'Has some local policeman decided to send you round asking questions? But yes – I have been staying with Maurice Tytherton.'

'And his death has disconcerted you?'

'Obviously. We are all – the small house-party here – very much upset. When a sudden death occurs, it seems natural to express proper condolences, and then pack up and go. But the police have asked us all to stay till tomorrow. And some of us may have to return for the inquest. Rather a bore, that. But my anxiety to assist the law is, of course, almost celebrated. I'm even perfectly willing to assist *you* – who may be described as the law in carpet slippers.'

'They may be useful for getting about quietly.' Appleby paused. 'There's plenty of room on this trunk, without any question of disagreeable contiguity. So won't you sit down?'

The man called Egon Raffaello sat down. Heaven knows his real name – Appleby reflected – but the ridiculous mix-up of his assumed one is almost offensively absurd. Perhaps Raffaello is still a common Italian name, although I don't remember ever having shaken anybody so denominated by the hand. And this chap is Portuguese. It's one of the few facts certainly known of him. Not even a political refugee – whom one might continue to respect even if he has been constrained to fall for a living on the more shady edge of things. Nothing to be said for him whatever.

But that's not true, Appleby thought. There's no human being on whom such a verdict should be pronounced. In this hostile universe some of us hold out longer or better than others, and in the eyes of the gods Egon Raffaello – who is a thorough-going pest in mine – is simply an early casualty. Which doesn't at all mean, however, that he ought to be let get away with something at other people's expense. So what is he doing here, anyway? One wouldn't suppose violence to be at all his line. Still, he must be checked out of the affair pretty thoroughly – whether by me or by Pride's men.

'Are you in the habit of visiting Elvedon?' Appleby asked.

'I've never been here before.' Raffaello produced a relaxed gesture. He was by nature an urbane twister, and his urbanity had been shaken only momentarily by his unexpected encounter with an old adversary. What he would in any case have to tell somebody sooner or later, he had no objection to telling Appleby now. 'And you'll want to know whether I came in a professional character. Well, certainly I did. Tytherton wanted to discuss one or two proposals at leisure. And to show me things.'

'Paintings?'

'Works of art in general. The collection here isn't at all remarkable, but it's worth thinking about, all the same.'

'From a commercial point of view? Tytherton was what may be called an investor in the fine arts?'

'My dear Appleby, they're all *that*.' Raffaello's tone was indulgent. 'No man in England knows that better than you. Think of all those dukes and marquises with Titians and Holbeins that you've hob-nobbed with in your time. Charming and unworldly characters. Removed through centuries of privilege from the base temptations of the market place. But was there ever one of them who didn't keep an eye on how such things were going?'

'Some of Tytherton's pictures went, I gather – and more or less out of the window. I imagine he had given up hope of recovering them. Was he perhaps proposing to make good the gaps by fresh purchases? And was he enlisting you to help him?'

'It's a reasonable conjecture, no doubt.' Raffaello smiled blandly. 'But matters of that sort are highly confidential, as you know. I could scarcely discuss them without the consent of Tytherton's heirs and executors.'

'Even when the manner of Tytherton's violent death is a matter of police investigation?'

'Well, well – we shall see about that. The day is still young, after all. By the way, it doesn't seem to have occurred to you that Tytherton may have wanted to *sell* something?'

'To sell something?' Appleby looked hard at Raffaello. He was wondering whether this question was as meaningless as its casual tone suggested, or whether it somehow represented Raffaello's vanity in some fashion betraying him. 'Tytherton was concerned to have a balanced and coherent collection? He sold off second-bests?'

'Another reasonable conjecture.' Raffaello stood up and stretched himself lazily in the sun. He appeared to have wholly recovered from the disconcerting apparition Appleby had constituted, and to be addressing himself to enjoying the situation. After all – Appleby thought grimly – he eluded me once. In fact he got the better of me. Why shouldn't he be confident he'll do it again?'

'Or he may have been hard up,' Raffaello said. 'Many of us are.'

'One wouldn't be prompted to such a notion by Elvedon, or by the way the place is maintained.'

'Perfectly true. But appearances can be deceptive in this sector of society.' Raffaello again made a sweeping gesture. 'It's a fact of which I've had a good deal of experience. One learns to look out for the signs.'

'And what are the signs here?'

'I see you haven't met Mrs Graves. Otherwise you'd scarcely ask.'

'I certainly haven't met Mrs Graves – or heard of her either.'

'And what about Carter? Coming to an understanding with him might be quite expensive, if you ask me. Miss Kentwell, of course, is different. A harmless creature, if there ever was one – although as tiresome as they come.'

'Do I understand that these people constitute a kind of house-party at Elvedon?'

'My dear Appleby, I see you are by no means *au courant*. Some of them I should call a little more than that. But you will see for yourself. My own advice to you would be to concentrate your celebrated detective powers on Catmull.'

'And who is Catmull?'

'The butler. It's never safe to ignore the butler. But, on reflection, I change my mind. Go not for Catmull but for his wife. Mrs Catmull is the cook. And if cuisine means anything, Mrs Catmull is the most sinister of the lot.'

Meaningless badinage, although not to be judged morally reprehensible, is seldom entertaining for long. Appleby remembered it now as one of this disagreeable character's more tiresome propensities. But there were more relevant matters to recall to memory. For example, there was Raffaello's chief field of professional activity. No doubt he had a good enough line on where to pick you up, say, a Caravaggio, if you wanted such a thing, and knew just where to find a couple of collectors susceptible of being talked into profitable competition with each other for a Monet or a Renoir. The mechanics of inflating a contemporary reputation at a commercially propitious moment were unlikely to be beyond him. And he certainly possessed skill in filtering quietly out of a private collection awkwardly valuable works on which no right-thinking man would like to see the successful collecting of estate duty. It was this last beneficent activity, indeed, that had first commended him to Appleby's notice a good many years ago. More recently, he had been peddling one or another remote past or dawn of history. He had a little gallery off Bond Street which announced in a refined and reticent lettering: *The Arts of the Ancient Orient*. He financed what had the appearance of a learned journal but really acted as a sales-sheet with the title *Etruria*. If you were knowledgeable, you went to him for authentic Etruscan stuff smuggled out of Italy, and got it; if you were less knowledgeable, you did the same thing, and acquired some perfectly respectable fakes. And then – Appleby remembered – there were the displaced llamas and monks and anchorites and archimandrites. These people were always turning up nowadays – fleeing from the threat of the sword, more or less, but with marketable objects of great value in their baggage, and stories about their own just proprietorship of these which nobody in the western world was in a position to check. Raffaello, it was understood, had cashed in on that.

Much of this was rather a long way from Elvedon Court. It did seem as if what might be called Raffaello's pliability had been his recommendation to the place; in other words, that the late Maurice Tytherton had been up to something not wholly reputable. People who get themselves murdered have often been up to precisely that. Roughly speaking, it is a black mark against a man if he finishes up with a bullet in brain or heart. Still, about Tytherton this remained wild surmise. He might well have been as monumentally respectable as most landowners, bankers, care-ridden industrialists, minor Ministers of the Crown, newspaper owners, and indeed all affluent persons normally are. As for the insinuations in one or two things Raffaello had said – well, that might just be the fellow's common venomous style. Except that one had to remember there had been the Reverend Mr Voysey as well. Voysey, who was odd but neither venomous nor vulgar, had been constrained to admit that a certain lack of edification marked the Elvedon scene. And who was Mrs Graves? Who was Carter? Could the significance of Mr and Mrs Catmull conceivably be other than a silly joke? Asking himself these questions now, Appleby had to confess to himself that he was hooked.

'What an estate agent would call an imposing country residence.' Raffaello had taken a few steps across the little glade to a point from which it was possible to glimpse the roof of Elvedon. He looked like a very minor devil, Appleby thought, taking a brooding and disparaging survey of Eden. 'Who inherits it? Not I'd suppose, that superior tart, the second Mrs Tytherton. The sponging nephew? Surely not. But I'm forgetting. There was a useless son, I've been told, by a first marriage. He skulks somewhere in South America.'

'On the contrary, he has the good fortune to be skulking within reach of your backside.'

These surprising words had scarcely been uttered before

28

Appleby was aware of Raffaello sprawling face-downward on the grass. It had been a vigorous and accurate kick. Had the unfortunate art dealer really been a football, he would have gone straight between the posts.

4

Nor was the assailant assuaged. He had taken up a threat-ening posture above the prone man.

'I don't know *who* you are,' he said. 'But *what* you are is clear enough. A poisonous little toad. Is that right?' He drew back one foot and swung it gently. 'Or shall I dribble you off the property?'

'Stop!' It had taken Appleby a moment to get on terms with this astonishing irruption. 'If you touch that man again you will find yourself under arrest.'

'And who the devil are you to give me orders?' The new arrival had swung round. 'Clear out.'

'I am, among other things, a Justice of the Peace. And I am not giving you orders. I am simply telling you, Mr Tytherton, of what will be the legal consequence of any further violence on your part.' Appleby paused. 'I suppose you know that your father is dead?'

'Yes.'

'Then consider the mere indecency, hard upon that, of becoming involved in a vulgar brawl.'

'It takes two to manage a brawl. This creature will simply take a leathering. Let me show you.'

'I'll sue you for assault. I'll have you shut up – put away. You're a madman.' Raffaello had picked himself up, seem-ingly not much injured, and managed to interpose Appleby between himself and the ferocious young man who was un-doubtedly Mark Tytherton.

'At least let me make him *say* he's a poisonous little toad.' Mark addressed this appeal to Appleby almost engagingly. 'It will take only a single clout. You'll see.'

'Mr Tytherton, you are not a schoolboy, and this is not a junior day-room. You no doubt overheard Mr Raffaello speak contemptuously both of yourself and others. But I advise you to forget about it, and think seriously of other things. I know little, so far, about the circumstances of your father's death. But they appear to have been mysterious, and anybody who may conceivably have been concerned will be required to give an account of himself.'

'What about that chap?' Contemptuously, Mark Tytherton pointed at Raffaello. 'How does he account for himself?'

'Mr Raffaello is an art-dealer, and has been staying at Elvedon as your father's guest.'

'And you – where do you come in?'

'I had better explain that at once.' And Appleby did so. 'So you understand,' he concluded, 'that I have no official standing in the affair whatever. But if the Chief Constable invites me to help, I shall do my best to do so.'

'I suppose you'll all want me to account for *my* movements?'

'Almost certainly.'

'And that will take some doing.' Raffaello interjected this viciously.

'At least we can tell this bloody wog to beat it for the time being?' Again Mark Tytherton appealed to Appleby. 'To crawl back into the woodwork?'

'Mr Raffaello may well wish to withdraw. Your childish and grossly insulting language, Mr Tytherton, is scarcely likely to induce him to linger.'

'A policeman, you say you are? You talk more like a book than a dick.' Mark had produced this with a grin which one might have interpreted either as ferocious or as good-humoured, according as to how one felt about him. 'Beetle off,' he added – almost amiably – to Raffaello.

'Don't worry. I'm going. If I come back, it will be with a van from the local madhouse.' And Egon Raffaello, who appeared to find Mark's juvenile form of wit catching, walked away.

'How did you know who I was?' There was uncompromising challenge in Mark Tytherton's voice, and he eyed Appleby warily.

'You more or less announced yourself, didn't you?'

'It was more than that. You weren't sufficiently surprised.'

'Wasn't I?' It amused Appleby that Mark had been dissatisfied with his *coup de théâtre*. 'As a matter of fact, I did already know you were around. You were spotted in the park a few days ago by the vicar.'

'Voysey?'

'Yes. He came to see your mother –'

'Step-mother.'

'Yes, of course. I beg your pardon. He came to Elvedon this morning, and was the first person I encountered. He told me how he had run into you.'

'Does he think I bolted from him?'

'He didn't suggest that to me. You simply hadn't noticed him.'

'No more I had.'

'Mr Tytherton, am I right in thinking that, even down to this present moment, you have let nobody at Elvedon know of your arrival in the neighbourhood?'

'Correct.'

'But you have heard of your father's death?'

'They were talking about it in my pub as I had breakfast.'

'They don't know who you are?'

'No. They're new people. They've taken over the pub since my last visit.'

'But have you registered with them under your own name?'

'Registered? Good Lord, it's a mere pot-house, and they don't bother about that kind of thing. The fellow just shouts to his wife that here's a gent who wants a room.'

'I see. But this pub must be frequented by people who remember you, and would recognize you?'

'Oh, yes – I suppose so. I didn't think about it.'

'You might have been detected at any time?'

'Detected?' There was bewilderment in Mark's voice. 'Oh, I see. This business of lurking and skulking. But it wasn't like that, at all – or not meant to be. My first idea was to come straight home. It would have been the rational thing. Fatted calf, and all that.'

'Do you regard yourself as very much a prodigal son?'

'You do ask damnably impertinent questions. But, well, no – I don't. It's true I last left England after a violent quarrel with my father –'

'Violence seems to be rather a thing with you, Mr Tytherton.'

'Violence?' Mark seemed momentarily at a loss. 'Oh, I see. That bastard's behind. He asked for it, didn't he?'

'Perhaps so. But may I suggest that, in the present state of affairs at Elvedon, a certain interest must attach to evidences of a propensity to violent behaviour?'

'They must have taught you to talk like that when you were a kid.' Mark Tytherton offered this impertinence cheerfully. 'But I see what you mean. If I had killed my father ...' Mark paused, and looked at Appleby with curiously wide-open eyes. 'It's a strange thing to have to say, isn't it? But if I *had* had another awful row with my father, and taken a gun or a chopper or whatever to him, I'd be rather unlikely, don't you think, to advertise what you call my propensity to violent behaviour just for the pleasure of booting some rotten dago on the bottom?'

'It's a point to consider, no doubt.' Appleby seemed not particularly impressed by the argument. 'Am I right in thinking that, when you were distracted by hearing the sound of talk in this spinney, and yielded to the pleasure of what is called, I believe, putting in the boot, you were in fact on your way to Elvedon to present yourself?'

'Yes, of course. And I've made a pretty fool of myself, haven't I? If I hadn't lost my nerve –'

'And lurked?'

'Just that. Put up in that pub and hung around before going through with the thing. If I hadn't done that, it seems possible that what has happened *wouldn't* have happened.'

'You mean, Mr Tytherton, that you have reason to believe that your father's death has been the consequence of a situation which your earlier arrival would have obviated?'

'Not specifically. I know nothing about my father's death. It's just a feeling that it all *might* have been different.'

'Different, exactly, from what?'

'I just mean that various things – things I don't myself know about at all – might have taken a different turn, so that he might have been alive now. Perhaps it's a silly feeling. But if I *had* gone up to the house at once – if I'd had the guts for it – then, because of the way one thing leads to another –' Mark broke off rather helplessly. 'It's difficult to explain.'

'I think you mean that your father's death has come at the end of a chain of events which you are entirely in the dark about – but which, even so, your turning up might have broken or altered.'

'That's just it.'

'Mr Tytherton, have you, whether directly or indirectly,

been getting very much news of your home during recent years?'

'Only in patches. This and that, you may say.'

'I see.' Appleby registered an impression that he had come on ground where Mark's instinct was for evasion. 'For instance, a business of stolen pictures a year or two ago. I dare say it may have got into the papers. You have heard about it?'

'Nothing at all. What you say is news to me entirely.'

'I haven't yet been given any particulars, but I gather none of the stolen works was recovered. Your father was judged to have taken it all rather quietly. But I'm not sure that he didn't have some hope of reviving the scent. I used to be a good deal concerned with such matters, and I rather suspect that my being brought to Elvedon by Colonel Pride this morning had some element of plot to it. At least I was to be asked to give advice.'

'And you think this has something to do with my father's death?'

'It would be rash to assert anything of the sort. But a possible link has to be kept in mind.'

'I say! Didn't you tell me that this disgusting chap Pulcinello –'

'Raffaello.'

'Yes. Didn't you say he was an art-dealer? Would there be anything in that?'

'I have far too little information to venture an opinion, but rather imagine I shall soon be given a good deal by Colonel Pride or his officers. And I'm going back to the house now. I take it you are going there too?'

'Well, I suppose so.' Mark Tytherton hesitated. 'I have to, I suppose – and I set out after breakfast to go through with it. But I don't know that I'll be a great success.'

'A success?' Appleby found himself wondering how much

this sudden diffidence was to be taken at its face value. 'My dear sir, are you not presumably at this moment the owner of the place?'

'I don't know. I haven't thought. You see, there's Alice – that's my step-mother. And there's my cousin Archie, who has always hung around. Or perhaps it's all going to be turned into a home for stray dogs.'

'Perhaps. But, whatever your relations with your father have been, the sober probability is that his sudden death has brought you a great deal of property.'

They walked out of the wood and through the garden in a silence which served to accentuate a monotonous cooing of doves behind them. The sound was like a bored or half-hearted keening for the dead.

'Were you brought up here?' Appleby asked.

'Oh, yes – all my boyhood. I was rather fond of it, as a matter of fact.'

'Aren't you fond of it any longer?'

'I suppose I ought to be. Perhaps I am. But I've wandered around, you know.' Mark Tytherton seemed almost confused. And suddenly he stopped in his tracks. 'I say, there's an ambulance! Do you think somebody else has got hurt?'

There was certainly an ambulance. It had taken the place of one of the police cars on the wide gravel expanse before the house.

'I think,' Appleby said gently, 'that it will have come for the body. The body must be taken away, you see, for the *post mortem*. That's routine. But it will be brought back before the funeral.'

'I see. But look – there's a kind of prison van as well!' Mark Tytherton glanced at Appleby in what might have been naive dismay. 'Who's *that* going to take away?'

'Your guess is as good as mine. Raffaello? Mrs Catmull

36

the cook? Actually, I expect it's here simply because the police piled into anything they had handy ... I beg your pardon!'

This apology was occasioned by Appleby's having turned rather sharply round a clipped hedge and almost stumbled over a lady sitting on a garden bench in its shade. But the lady was not discomposed.

'Not at all,' she said. 'It seems almost wrong that it should be so beautiful a morning, but I have come out to enjoy it, all the same. I think you must be Sir John Appleby? Mr Ramsden – poor Mr Tytherton's secretary – was told about you by the military man. I didn't catch his name.'

'Colonel Pride. He's the Chief Constable.'

'Ah, yes. And Mr Ramsden told me. My name is Jane Kentwell, and I have been staying in the house over the past few days. I cannot claim to be more than an acquaintance of the Tythertons.' There was a pause which seemed designed to lend a slight emphasis to this remark. 'But I am much shocked by what has happened, all the same. And you' – Miss Kentwell had turned politely to Mark – 'are Maurice Tytherton's son. Will you allow me to say how grieved I am, and how much I wish to sympathize?'

Perhaps because of his life in exotic parts, Mark appeared a shade thrown out of his stride by this business of a competent English gentlewoman doing her stuff.

'Thank you very much,' he said gruffly. 'But I can't see how you know me from Adam, I must say.'

'Your photograph stands on your father's desk – in his small writing-room, where he died.' Miss Kentwell paused, apparently out of a well-bred impulse to mute what might easily be too dramatic a note. 'You may like to think that it was the last thing he ever saw.'

5

Whether Mark Tytherton did like to think this was not clear. Perhaps he considered Miss Kentwell's suggestion – coming, as it did, from a total stranger – an indecent invasion of family privacy. Certainly his response was no more than an inarticulate grunt, coupled with a movement as if to walk on. Miss Kentwell, however, had more to say.

'I have been so interested to hear about your work in South America. It is clear that you have had to undertake substantial responsibilities from an early age.'

'That's all rubbish – the kind of thing you say about the wanderer from the fold. I've just been doing this and that.'

'I am sure that you are taking too modest a view of yourself.' Miss Kentwell spoke firmly, and as a woman who expects to be believed. Raffaello, Appleby recalled, had pronounced a modified eulogy upon her as a harmless creature of a tiresome sort, and at the moment at least her tiresomeness was evident. 'But now,' she continued, 'there is suddenly this larger sphere of usefulness before you. You will have the happiness of bringing some of your father's finest schemes to fruition.'

'I hope I'm going to have the happiness of keeping out of quod. My father has been done in, and now the dicks have found me hiding in the wood-shed. It doesn't look too good, does it?'

This odd and indecorous speech did for a moment hold

Miss Kentwell up. Yet almost at once she returned to the charge.

'You must not distress yourself, Mr Tytherton, with morbid fancies. They are common in the first shock of bereavement. But they quickly pass, particularly if one throws oneself at once into some wide sphere of usefulness, some well conceived scheme of beneficent activity.'

It was at this point that Appleby felt the character of Miss Kentwell to be coming clear. She was a fanatical promoter of good works, and she felt that somebody freshly in command of what must be presumed a large fortune was a prospect to be gone for at once. It was even possible that she had softened up the late Maurice Tytherton in the interest of some charitable project or other, and was now beginning to mount a campaign to ensure his son's carrying it on. Appleby judged this something of a forlorn hope. Certainly Mark Tytherton was responding far from amiably now.

'I must be getting on to the house,' he said abruptly. 'Only decent to see Alice, I suppose.' This remark he had addressed to Appleby. 'Hope you won't be obliged to hang around Elvedon indefinitely.' This had been for Miss Kentwell. 'So long.' And on this colloquial note Mark Tytherton strode away.

'A most interesting young man.' Miss Kentwell had somehow managed to take it for granted that Appleby would remain in conversation with her. 'His manner is a little unpolished, but that is merely a matter of his colonial associations. I believed him destined to be a person of strong character and vigorous conviction.'

'Possibly so. But by the way, and talking of his colonial associations, you didn't seem at all surprised at his having suddenly turned up here.'

'It would have been scarcely civil, Sir John, to betray any

reaction of that kind. One is only sorry that he didn't arrive a few days earlier. He might have cheered and heartened his father's last hours.'

'His father didn't exactly have last hours of that sort.'

'Perfectly true. For a moment I was forgetting the extremely distressing circumstances of Mr Tytherton's end. A death without a deathbed is a horrid thing.' Miss Kentwell paused on this curiously Victorian sentiment. 'Unless,' she added as an afterthought, 'it be death on the field of battle. That is quite another matter.'

'It appears so to us. To the people dying, I suppose, these distinctions may not be all that apparent.'

'That is a most interesting thought.' It was evident that Miss Kentwell was not readily made aware of any element of levity in response to her observations. 'I am so glad that the young man is going straight to Mrs Tytherton. As you can well imagine, she is prostrated. The presence of her step-son will be a great support to her.'

'No doubt – although I can't see that they can be very well known to each other. Would you describe the Tythertons, incidentally, as a devoted couple?'

'Ah.' Miss Kentwell made this noise in a considering way, and was plainly playing for time. It must be her instinct to treat as scandalous any suggestion that couples – at least among the respectable classes – are ever other than devoted. On the other hand, and in this instance, it looked as if there was something to a contrary effect that she wanted to say. And she managed to say it now. 'One could not maintain, Sir John, that poor Mr Tytherton's second marriage quite filled all his horizons.' Miss Kentwell paused on this expansive if not very lucid image. 'Upon signs of that, indeed, one might come in the composition of our present small house-party.'

'Indeed?'

'And of the second marriage there are, of course, no children.' Miss Kentwell had gone discreetly off on another tack. 'So it seemed rather a question of Mr Tytherton's finding new fields of interest, of worthwhile interest. Signs were not wanting that he was about to do so.'

'I see.' Appleby felt prompted to add: 'You think you had pretty well nobbled him for something?' Instead, he said: 'I gather he had been something of a collector or connoisseur of pictures, and so on. Perhaps he was proposing to start in again on that? Perhaps that's why Mr Raffaello is here?'

'Mr Tytherton was too large a man to rest content with a sterile dilettantism.' Miss Kentwell paused on this elevated persuasion. 'Besides, Sir John, as you know, in that field public recognition takes some time to mature. To give this to one gallery and that to another is not enough. A whole collection is required, and the nation itself has to be the recipient. All that takes time.'

'I suppose it does.' Appleby was conscious of perceptible effort as required for dissimulating a growing astonishment before this lady. 'Would you describe the dead man as having been a person of the first ability?'

'Not, I think, *quite* that.'

'He wouldn't have been likely, for example, to have got to the Lords on a life peerage by way of public service on boards and commissions and so on? Philanthropy would have to be his line? What one might call instant philanthropy, if possible?'

'I am afraid we are coming to speak in very crude terms, Sir John. Of course Mr Tytherton would have accepted proper public recognition of anything he did. But his deeper motive –'

'Quite so. We need waste no time upon so obvious a thought. However – and to be crude again for just a moment

– are you sure that there was quite all that money available?'

'No, I am not.' Miss Kentwell was surprisingly emphatic. 'I am bound to confess that my inquiries in that direction have yielded some rather disappointing, even disconcerting, results. However, we must not talk in this fashion with poor Mr Tytherton not yet even in his grave. I am told that the coroner's inquest is likely to be held on Thursday. It is most inconvenient, since it will clash with an important meeting – that of the committee of the Society for the Relief of Depressed Widows of the Higher Clergy. There is a need there that is too little recognized. So I am most anxious to attend.'

'Then I hope you will be able to do so. Have you been positively notified that you will be required to give evidence at the inquest?'

'But of course, Sir John!' Miss Kentwell sounded surprised and even offended. 'Was I not the first person to set eye upon the body?'

'Dear me! I am sorry to hear that. It must have been a most distressing experience.' The facts of the case, Appleby thought, were coming to him all out of order and in an almost luxuriously amateur way. He would have been perfectly happy pottering round Elvedon all day, simply picking up here and there pleasing pieces of information like this. Being closeted with one of Pride's senior men and presented with a well ordered narrative wouldn't be half the fun.

'Thank you, yes – it was most distressing. It is probably best that dead bodies should be found by servants. They are less sensitive, and therefore less easily upset.'

'Dead bodies are very frequently found by butlers,' Appleby said gravely. 'That is perhaps the best arrangement. Butlers are phlegmatic. They preserve an impassive demeanour in midst of the most trying circumstances. However, it was not as bad as it might have been. For I can perceive, Miss Kentwell, that you are a strong-minded woman. I believe you may even be possessed of what is called an iron nerve.'

'Really, Sir John, I would hardly claim –'

'Think if it had been, say, the depressed widow of a higher clergyman who discovered Mr Tytherton's corpse. The poor soul would have had hysterics on the spot.' Appleby pulled himself up. Being an amateur was going to his head, as these irresponsible and scandalous witticisms showed. And he mustn't let a rash frivolity offend Miss Kentwell. 'And were you by yourself,' he asked, 'when you made the discovery?'

'Not exactly. I was with Mr Ramsden. But, naturally, he had opened the door for me, and allowed me to pass in first.'

'In fact, you were ushered in on the corpse?'

'That is an odd way of expressing it, Sir John. But perfectly accurate.'

'Then, I take it –' Appleby broke off, his eye having been caught by a small stir of activity in front of the house. The ambulance was driving up to the foot of the steps leading to the front door. It was doing this at a crawl, as if the driver was conscious of being involved in what was in fact the first stage of a funeral. Several people had emerged from the house, and were standing awkwardly in a line, as if for some muted formal occasion. Appleby recognized only Pride, Mark Tytherton, and Catmull the butler – a circumstance persuading him that, if he was really going to be involved in the affair, the time had come to stop wandering round its periphery. And now the body had appeared, swathed and on a stretcher. There was a pause for some sort of consultation about getting it down to ground-level.

Appleby had sat down beside Miss Kentwell, and he now felt something uncomfortable about this species of spectatorship from a middle distance. Maurice Tytherton was leaving home. Appleby, after a fashion, was his guest. It would be only decent to participate in this leave-taking.

'I think I'll walk over,' he said.

'Then let me not detain you, Sir John. I shall remain here – but with the serious thoughts such an occasion suggests.' And Miss Kentwell offered Appleby a composed bow.

The stretcher and its burden were already being got into the ambulance when he reached the near side of the gravel sweep. So he simply stood and watched the doors being closed on it. He rather supposed he had no wish himself to view the body, although no doubt it would be available for the purpose in some proper place. And there would be plenty of photographs – the grim sort of photographs that are never seen except by policemen and lawyers and the unfortunate members of juries. Perhaps among the group of people who had come indecisively down the steps and were now standing pointlessly at the foot of them there was somebody who was going to study the faces of a jury from the dock. Perhaps it was all as good as determined already; just what had happened was by now known to every policeman in the house; tomorrow's newspapers would inform a not very curious world that this or that individual at Elvedon was 'assisting the police in their inquiries'.

The very phrase, Appleby told himself, had been invented since his time – which was why he didn't like it. And now he watched the ambulance drive away, and the knot of mourners or spectators or whatever they were to be called begin to climb the steps again. He noticed the absurd circumstance that Catmull was carrying a neatly folded travelling-rug. It had been part of the regular ritual of seeing his employer off the premises, no doubt, and he had automatically gone through with it on the present occasion.

44

Only Tommy Pride was left – and Tommy was signalling to him urgently, was striding across the gravel, had taken him by the arm.

'My dear John, I was afraid you had found means to quit the place. Walk in the grounds, eh? Delightful morning for it. But now, for the Lord's sake, come in and have a word about this damnable business. Of course I haven't positively promised Henderson –'

'Who is Henderson?'

'My senior man on this criminal side of things. Thoroughly agreeable, unassuming fellow. As I say, I wouldn't in the least put you in a false position. We came across in a purely social way –'

'Did we? Wasn't there – honestly, Tommy – some notion that I might talk to Tytherton about his stolen pictures?'

'Well, yes – as a matter of fact I suppose there was. But that's all blown sky-high now. Poor fellow's gone where pilfered Poussins are not, eh? Well, as I was saying, I don't remotely want to –'

'Tommy, if I'm coming in on this thing, don't let me give the impression of being dragged in screaming. Treat me as straining at the leash. It will feel nicer that way.'

'My dear fellow, I knew I could count on you.' Pride was at once delicately uneffusive. 'Let's go inside.'

They mounted the steps together. There was still a constable at the front door, and the saluting business was gone through with again. Pride seemed to feel that he ought to apologize for it.

'Odd thing,' he said. 'I find myself not liking them doing that quite so smartly. Don't approve of the police going para-military. Old-style copper, bringing his finger to his helmet in any wandering way he fancied, much more my idea of the thing. Don't want Wellington Barracks all over

45

again. But of course one has to keep such outmoded feelings under one's hat.'

'Very prudent.'

'Don't much care for having a chap at the door like that, either. Army of occupation, eh? But one has to think of the reporters and press-photographers, you know. They'll be turning up any time now – all assurance and B.B.C. English and old school ties. You have to have a stout fellow at the gate, or the impertinent bastards are all over the place. Of course it's their living, poor devils. When I see them retreat baffled, I feel I've denied them a square meal.'

'That's very compassionate of you.'

'But, John, I think I ought to warn you.' They were now in Elvedon's imposing hall again, and Pride had lowered his voice – less at being impressed by the surrounding splendours, perhaps, than from a realistic sense of their treacherous acoustic properties. 'It may be rather a nasty business.'

'Nasty?'

'Sexual.' Pride had lowered his voice still further, so that Appleby had a momentary dim vision of unspeakable depravities. 'Spot of adultery going on here, it seems. Not a decent thing in a private house, at all. A hotel the place for that sort of thing among honest people, eh? Sorry to say it. But the whole damned mansion smells to me of pretty poor form.'

6

They went straight to the room in which Maurice Tytherton had died. Or in which – to make an elementary point – the dead body of Maurice Tytherton had been found. Since Elvedon was no Blenheim or Castle Howard, one consequence of its over-imposing hall had been the hoisting of a number of rooms of principal consequence up to the first floor. This seemed to Appleby to produce a slight sense of muddle, and must certainly conduce, as in a town house, to a good deal of laborious trotting up and down stairs. But as the main staircase was a singularly daring and graceful circular affair of finely poised masonry, perhaps that was no hardship. For footmen and housemaids of an earlier age, toiling with water, coal, and refreshment whether light or heavy on more constricted arteries virtually buried within a wall, it must have been a different matter. But then servants (as the philanthropic Miss Kentwell had remarked) are by a wise dispensation of providence created less sensitive than their employers. In this present age there was presumably a certain amount of mechanical conveyance in the form of hoists or lifts.

What Tytherton had called, it seemed, his workroom was on the first floor, and looked down on the terrace before the south front of the house. It wasn't particularly large or elaborately furnished, but this made all the more striking the fact that over the mantelpiece there was something really splendid: a threequarter-length portrait of a nobleman by Goya.

Appleby noticed it with a start of surprise which had nothing to do with the late Maurice Tytherton and his affairs. He had owned a much-prized colour-print of it as a boy – at which time, he seemed to remember, the original had been in the possession of the Duke of Horton. Tytherton must have acquired it at the great sale at Scamnum. He must have been quite a high-flying collector if he went in for that sort of thing.

But now Inspector Henderson had begun his narrative. He was, as Pride had said, an unassuming man, with plenty of experience which had yet not, perhaps, taken him into the neighbourhood of quite this kind of thing before. He addressed himself to Appleby, since what he had to say the Chief Constable was already familiar with.

'What we have, sir, is a big house full of valuable things, where a moderately successful burglary is known to have been carried out a couple of years ago. Plenty left for all comers, if they care to have a go at it. So I drive up with this in my head, you may say, when I get word that the owner has been shot dead in the middle of the night.'

'The middle of the night?'

'Thank you, sir. Perhaps a misleading expression. Late at night: some time after eleven o'clock.'

'It sounds a little early for a burglary, even in the country.'

'I quite agree. But I do have to have the possibility of robbery – of Mr Tytherton surprising one kind of thief or another, say – in my head from the start. It tells me I must waste no time before trying to discover whether anything notable is in fact missing, and whether there are signs of any breaking in. In a sense, you may say, the relations of the various people in the house will keep. But time may be of the essence of stopping valuable property from disappearing for good.'

'Very true, Inspector. Any results?'

'Entirely negative, so far. No positive sign of breaking and entering. But it's not easy to arrive at certainty there when you're dealing with a large place like Elvedon. Even without an accomplice in the house, a thief might well be able to prospect a means of entrance which it might take us quite some time to tumble to.'

'Not a doubt about that. And the question of missing property?'

'We've worked hard, but it's early days to say. Elvedon's not like a suburban villa, that you can check over with the owner or his wife in fifteen minutes. Then again, you see, there's the question of who really knows.'

'Walking inventory, eh?' Colonel Pride interjected.

'Quite so, sir. Mrs Tytherton seems the likeliest person to be well informed in the matter, but it wouldn't be quite the thing to badger her about the details of the Elvedon pictures and porcelain and so on just at the moment.'

'Absolutely right, Henderson. Very proper. Give her a chance.'

'Then there's the butler, Catmull. He has checked over what he calls his own province – meaning silver, and the like. He seems quite sound on that, and reports everything present and correct. But I can't call him very co-operative over the larger scene.'

'I see.' Appleby considered. 'What about Tytherton's secretary – Ramsden, isn't he called?'

'Yes, indeed. He's quite a young man, but seems to have lived at Elvedon for a good many years. Has the whole place under his thumb, if you ask me.'

'What's that?' The Chief Constable was alerted. 'In some sinister way, do you mean?'

'Not exactly, sir. But I have a feeling that he has gathered into his own hands rather more control of things than he cares to make evident. And he has been helpful enough. The valuable pictures, like this one on the wall here, are scattered around the house without too much regard to security. Mr Ramsden made a check which I could see was thoroughly well-informed and efficient. And he finds nothing missing.'

'So it rather looks,' Appleby said, 'as if Elvedon's unfortunate proprietor didn't perish in defending his possessions against marauders?'

'At a first glance, yes. But from the first, of course, I've had to think in terms of other possibilities as well.'

'Suicide, for example.'

'Yes, sir.' Henderson gave Appleby a swift glance, perfectly aware that he was, in a sense, being tested out. 'I don't rule out suicide as being involved.'

'Suicide? God bless my soul!' The Chief Constable was impatient. 'Every inch of this room has been searched. Do you suggest that the poor chap first shot himself and then swallowed the revolver?'

'No I don't,' Appleby said. 'But people have performed feats almost as remarkable in order to conceal the fact that they have made away with themselves. Remember *Thor Bridge*.'

'What the devil is that?'

'I see that the Inspector can tell you.'

'One of the Sherlock Holmes stories, sir.' Henderson smiled a shade indulgently. 'The gun is tied to a stone, which is hung over the bridge. When it is let go –'

'It is whipped over the parapet and into the river.' Appleby had walked over to the window, opened it, and was looking out. 'Only, it takes a tell-tale chip out of the parapet ... Look at Hermes, Tommy.'

Reluctantly, Pride looked at Hermes – a much-weathered statue on a pedestal immediately below.

'On this occasion,' Appleby went on, 'the chip may have been taken out of his skull, wouldn't you say?'

'Absolute nonsense.'

'I'm afraid so.' Appleby closed the window. 'But the general point is valid. People have committed suicide and gone to strange and ingenious lengths to obscure the fact. People have committed suicide and *other* people have promptly undertaken the same obscuration on their behalf. Or there was the episode I think of as *The Case of X, Y, and Z*. It sounds like one of Holmes's, but I assure you it was one of my own. X killed himself, and when Y found the body he so arranged matters that Z was in danger of being convicted of murder. And all three may be described as having moved in good society.' Appleby turned back into the room and sat down. 'So one can't too closely scrutinize one's facts. Shall we begin?'

'I think that should mean with the discovery of the body.' Henderson had produced a notebook. 'It took place in this room at approximately twenty past eleven last night, and the immediate circumstances were as follows. *First*: there was a small house party, only two members of which, a Mr Raffaello and a Miss Kentwell, were at all unfamiliar with the place. *Second*: Mr Tytherton excused himself to his guests round about ten o'clock and for some time the party appears to have drifted about a little restlessly here and there. *Third*: later on, the secretary, Ramsden, came in to join them, and noticed that Raffaello, who had been drinking, was making a bit of a nuisance of himself towards a woman called Mrs Graves. I get the impression that keeping an eye on embarrassments of this sort, and taking appropriate tactful action, is more or less part of Ramsden's job.'

'Odd state of affairs,' the Chief Constable said. 'Deplorable, eh?'

'So Ramsden suggested that he should show Raffaello and Miss Kentwell – the comparative strangers, as I've said

51

– one of the sights of the place. One of its nocturnal sights, you might say. You climb to the lantern on the roof, and on any clear moonlight night there's a magnificent view.

'Now, *Fourth*: this plan only partly fulfilled itself. Raffaello, who was more or less breathing down Mrs Graves's cleavage – Mr Ramsden's words these, sir – turned down the invitation out of hand, with the result that Ramsden was left stuck with Miss Kentwell, who was all in favour of the expedition. So he had to lead her away to no particular purpose. But he is a very gentlemanlike young man, and he seems to have done the thing in style, politely showing off this and that as they made their way to the top of the house. *Fifth*: the party as left downstairs broke up almost at once. Nobody has been willing to tell me much about this, but I think it possible that Mrs Graves – a very smart woman, she is, very fashionable indeed, sir – had to go off to bed to end Raffaello's nonsense, and that then everybody else did the same. The feeling I get is that there was something uncommonly uncomfortable, or edgy, about the whole evening.'

'Dubious crowd,' Colonel Pride said. 'It becomes clearer and clearer. Eh, John? Oughtn't to have proposed to land you in it.'

'*Sixth*: this dispersal was, from our point of view, neatly and awkwardly complete. There was nobody without his or her own room; and off they all went into privacy. And they remained like that until the murder – perhaps one had better say the fatality – was discovered.'

'All,' Appleby said, 'except Ramsden and Miss Kentwell, innocently seeking, hand in hand, certain glimpses of the moon.'

'Just so, sir. And, as you will realize in a moment, they are the only people with an alibi. You might say they hand each other alibis.'

'Deuced fishy,' Pride said.

'Well, sir, it can be viewed that way. Put very formally, Mr Tytherton's death may have been brought about by any single person in this house, with the exception of these two. These two would have to be conspirators.'

'And what's more likely. Eh, John?' Colonel Pride might have been described as hot on the scent.

'They sound an improbable couple. But it's a possibility, I agree.' Appleby paused. 'But, Inspector, we've lost sight of the movements of the dead man. Not that dead men do move.'

'No, sir.' Henderson had received this witticism with civil respect. '*Seventh*: I have something fairly specific on the movements of the two people we've been discussing. On their way to the top of the house they came into this room – partly, it seems, to tell Mr Tytherton what they were about, and suggest he go up to the roof with them.'

'And partly, would you say, to show Miss Kentwell this Goya? But, come to think of it, I doubt whether she much approved her host's activities as a collector. She had other plans for him.'

'That's rather what Mr Ramsden hints at.' Henderson was impressed. 'Anyway, they came in here, where Ramsden supposed his employer would be working. The lights were on, but there was no sign of him. So they waited for a minute or two, and came away again. Ramsden says he supposed Tytherton had gone to the lavatory. He says he had a notion that Miss Kentwell supposed the same thing, and was embarrassed by it. Anyway, off they went again, and climbed to the leads.'

'I suppose there really was a moon?'

'The moon isn't one of the doubtful factors, sir. It was a beautiful night.'

7

'Then I don't doubt the view was worth inspecting.' Appleby had got to his feet again and returned to the window. He felt restless and knew why: this was the stage in an affair at which he wanted to get past the reports of competent subordinates and enjoy a run for his own money. But the immediate prospect didn't conduce to bustle. A peacock had appeared and perched on the head of Hermes just below; it half spread out its tail as Appleby watched; then seemed to think better of the effort, and simply reposed in the sun. What was visible of the park was at present given over to a few head of cattle of a congruously superior sort. The tower of what must be Mr Voysey's church stood off behind a belt of trees – hovering, one might say, to proffer its services if required, but without any disrespectful importunity. There was a little ripple on a corner of the lake. It was hard to extract from those appearances any effect of an imperative call to action. Appleby now spoke briskly, all the same.

'Well, those two people went up to the roof. For how long?'

'Long enough to smoke a cigarette.' Henderson had consulted his notebook. 'Ramsden's words.'

'Any proof that they *did* go there? Were they noticed by a servant – anything of that kind?'

'No. They simply corroborate each other's story.'

'What about the cigarettes?'

'Quite so, sir.' Henderson was prepared for this question.

'I found two butts on the leads myself – quite fresh, and of the kind Ramsden appears to carry around with him. They weren't beside what's called the lantern – which is no more than a rather grand skylight – but over in the north-west corner of the roof of the main building. And that corresponds with what they remember of their movements. The lantern is on an octagonal platform some feet higher than the rest of the roof. They climbed to that first, and then came down and circled the whole perimeter of the place, more or less close to the enclosing balustrade. Ramsden, still doing the host's right-hand man, pointed out various landmarks. Then they descended by a second staircase, and more or less wandered back through the house and to this room.'

'And then came the crunch?'

'Just that. I get a feeling that Miss Kentwell was losing no opportunity of making herself agreeable to Mr Tytherton, and was proposing to say good night, if he was back in his workroom. That, and polite remarks about her little tour, no doubt. Anyway, for the second time within about twenty minutes, young Mr Ramsden ushered her in. And there' – with an unexpected effect of drama, Inspector Henderson's finger shot out and pointed at a writing-table – 'the dead man lay sprawled.'

'Shocking thing,' Colonel Pride said. 'A lady, I mean, being confronted with such a sight. Sounds a tiresome woman, I admit. Kind of professional sponger on the rich in the interest of large charities. Works on commission, likely enough. Odd, eh? Sorry for her, all the same. Unless, of course, these two really are the villains of the piece. Mustn't lose sight of the notion. But it's hard to see what interest they could have in common.'

'Quite so, sir.' Henderson had received these remarks respectfully. 'And I suppose it's possible that enquiry will reveal some concealed association. At the moment, however, I confess to seeing several more promising avenues.'

'Then let us press on with them, my dear chap.'

'Certainly, sir. But first I had better tell Sir John about the period immediately succeeding the discovery. This young Mr Ramsden seems to have behaved very efficiently – and the first efficient thing he did was to look at his watch. It was exactly eleven-twenty.'

'I see.' Appleby frowned suddenly. 'Inspector, let me get this right. The *first thing*? Do you mean that Ramsden followed Miss Kentwell into this room, saw that his employer had been shot dead, or nearly dead – and *instantly looked at his watch*?'

'Just that. He made a point of being precise about it to me.'

'By way of airing or showing off his efficiency?'

'No, sir. He realizes the oddity of it, as a matter of fact. He says he has an instinct to be precise about time, and that it must have made him do this automatic thing. Incidentally there can have been no rational occasion to suppose that Tytherton was only, as you put it, nearly dead. The state of his head told only one story. Nevertheless, the order in which Ramsden at once proceeded was undoubtedly the correct one. He picked up the telephone on the writing-table and called the Tythertons' doctor, who lives no more than a couple of miles away. Then he put through a 999 call to the police. And then he poured Miss Kentwell some brandy.'

'Very proper attention,' Colonel Pride said approvingly. 'Knocked out, was she?'

'It's my impression she didn't fall into any panic, but that she was bewildered and in a slight state of shock. Ramsden then went over to that other telephone – the one beside the fireplace. It's a house telephone, and he called up the butler on it. Name of Catmull, you will remember, sir. He told

Catmull what had happened, and ordered him to get his wife out of bed if necessary, and come to the workroom at once. They were both still up, it seems, and came straight away. Ramsden told Mrs Catmull to stay with Miss Kentwell, and Catmull to be ready to admit the doctor and the police. After that, Ramsden made his way to Mrs Tytherton's room, and broke the news to her. The doctor was here by twenty-five to twelve, and a couple of my men arrived a few minutes later. I myself turned up just before midnight' – Henderson smiled faintly – 'with a safety-razor in my pocket.'

'Wise precaution.' Colonel Pride nodded approvingly. 'Always encourage a smart turn-out, eh?'

'Undoubtedly.' Appleby, to whom the question had been addressed, turned to Henderson. 'When you put the razor in one pocket,' he asked, 'I don't suppose you balanced it with a revolver in the other?'

'Certainly I didn't.' Henderson's tone was almost reproving. 'I had no notion of running into a gang of armed robbers, or anything of that kind.'

'It wasn't all that unlikely, Inspector – not with affairs like that around.' Appleby pointed to the Goya. 'But I was really thinking of something else: a harmless, although perhaps mildly alarming experiment. Just a pot shot at nothing in particular, taken in the quiet of midnight or thereabout in this room. Wouldn't it make a bit of a rumpus? I'm surprised that, so far, I've heard nothing about the sound of a shot.'

'Well, sir, there is something on the record there, and I'll be coming to it in a moment.' Henderson was unperturbed. 'It's more perplexing than helpful, to my mind. However, there are three preliminary points to make. The first is that a great house like this is a very solid affair. A pistol-shot won't necessarily sound like the crack of doom in it, as it would in a small villa. Then, again, there's the character and calibre of the weapon used. We have no report on that as yet, but at the point-blank range involved the ugly job could have been done with something pretty well like a toy – the sort of miniature weapon ladies whip out of neat little handbags in movies. Not much bite, but even less bark. And the third point is this: almost up to the moment of dispersing and going to bed, the party downstairs seems to have been amusing itself every now and then with intermittent bursts of loud music – pop music, it seems – from an affair like a domestic juke-box.'

'Good heavens!' The Chief Constable made an expressive gesture. 'A thoroughly rackety crowd. Ashamed, my dear John, that I thought of introducing you to them.'

'On the contrary, Tommy, I can hardly wait to make their acquaintance. But, Inspector, you say there is some record about hearing a possible shot?'

'Yes, sir. From a Mr Archibald Tytherton. I don't think I've had occasion to mention him.'

'But I have,' Colonel Pride said. 'You remember, John? Nephew of Tytherton's who comes and goes, and seems not on record as doing much else. What was he doing last night, Henderson? Coming and going, I shouldn't be surprised.' And Pride chuckled, much pleased at thus refreshing the company with wit.

'Well, sir, he certainly went. Rather early, it seems. Even before his uncle went off to write letters, or whatever it was supposed to be. He went to bed. He's quite frank about it.'

'Frank?' There was resigned acceptance of scandal in Pride's tone. 'You mean he went shamelessly off to bed with one of the women?'

'No, sir – or not so far as he has admitted, or I know.' Henderson had turned warily wooden before this guileless admission of the possibility of disorderly courses on the part of persons of consideration in the county. 'Mr Archibald Tytherton's frankness was on the score of inebriety. He had been drinking too much from early in the evening. It was on account of his having had a dispute with his uncle. It had unsettled him.'

'Just a moment, Inspector.' Appleby was now prowling almost uneasily around the death-chamber in which this conference was taking place. 'Did he produce this story of a dispute with Maurice Tytherton off his own bat? No – that's not quite what I mean. Were its circumstances such that it might have escaped the record altogether if he hadn't mentioned it himself?'

'I rather gather not, sir. There had been a witness of at least some part of it. But the young man says he was most attached to his uncle, so that this little flare-up upset him very much.'

'And sent him to the bottle?'

'Yes, sir. Or to the decanters, perhaps one ought to say.'

'My dear Henderson' – Colonel Pride's ear for irony was not of the finest – 'alk is alk, whatever it arrives in. The fellow got tight, and had the grace to take himself off?'

'Just that. And it seems that, when fairly drunk, he goes off to sleep the moment his head touches the pillow. An enviable physiological predisposition.'

'No doubt. So he went straight to sleep?'

'So he says – but with a complete inability to name a likely hour. He seems not to have Mr Ramsden's habit of taking an informative look at his watch. What he next reports is a nightmare.'

'An informative nightmare?' Appleby asked.

'Well, that's what he suggests. He was rather proud of producing it. He says he had a dream in which he was playing billiards.'

'What's nightmarish about that?' the Chief Constable inquired. 'Boring occupation, I've always felt. But nothing alarming about it.'

'The billiard-table kept growing larger and larger, he says. So did the cues. And the balls were eventually like cannon-balls, and he had to keep on banging them around for dear life. The noise was like a breaking-up of icebergs.' Inspector Henderson paused appreciatively. 'Rather a graphic touch, that.'

'And then,' Appleby said, 'one particularly resounding crack woke him up, and he thought it might have been a revolver-shot? Is that the story?'

'Not quite. It didn't, that is, occur to him at the time, but swam up in his memory again when I was questioning him. It's a way one does remember dreams.'

'True enough. And it's popularly supposed that one builds into them at times external stimuli registered in the instant of waking. But if he has no notion of when this supposed happening took place – as I gather is the fact – then it seems unlikely to help us very much. Does he believe himself to have gone to sleep again?'

'He thinks he dozed off. Catmull got him out of bed just before midnight, but doesn't know whether he was asleep. Catmull thought proper to arouse the whole household, apart from such servants as there are. Sensible enough. It meant people were more or less on parade when we wanted them.'

'Ah, yes – servants. Just how does the household run?'

'Through a good part of the year it appears to be a modified week-end affair. The Catmulls and Ramsden are the only permanent – that's to say, continuous – residents. There's a house, or flat, in town, with another Catmull as a fixture in it.'

'Do you mean a brother of this fellow?'

'No, sir – just another manservant of the same standing. What else there is, apart from outdoor people, is a few Italian maidservants who shuttle to and fro in the wake of their employers.'

'Quite an *entourage*,' Pride said. 'Deuced expensive, too. Money there, I suppose. But one wonders. Henderson, is it your immediate impression that Mrs Tytherton would be a woman with extravagant tastes?'

'Oh, decidedly – by what I think of as ordinary standards, sir. Ordinary wealthy people's standards, that is. Drives her own Rolls, and nobody else let near it. Nothing too staggering in that, perhaps. But indicative, in a manner of speaking.'

'I've heard things to the same effect, I'm bound to say. Come to think of it, met her at dinner at old Lady Killcanon's some time ago, absolutely dripping diamonds. Might have been proposing to dominate the grand ball of the season. Not really the thing. Tytherton a bit hard-pressed, I shouldn't be surprised. If you have a wife like that, it's unfortunate to have a taste for buying Goyas and what-not as well. However, poor chap won't be hard-pressed in the grave, eh? Not even literally, so to speak. Slap-up mausoleum just over the hill. Airy and commodious, I believe. No crush of ancestors as yet ... By jove! Twelve o'clock.'

8

It was certainly noon. The fact had been signalized at some middle distance by the unassuming chime of a stable clock. And exactly on the last stroke, with something of the effect of an expensive automaton, the door of the late Maurice Tytherton's workroom flew open, and a newcomer stood framed in it. It was a woman, and although she wasn't at the moment dripping diamonds Appleby found himself without the slightest doubt as to her identity.

Here was a principal personage of the drama at last – Alice Tytherton, widow of the dead man. She had every right thus to march straight in, yet she had done so with a hint of challenge which for a moment left the three men standing alerted before her. But then men must often have stood before her like that, either aroused or alarmed by an uncommonly handsome woman so manifestly capable of designs of the most predatory sort. If one had to live in a jungle, Appleby told himself, it would probably be sensible to compound with the whole system of savage nature, and take on a mate like this. In civilized conditions she might turn out an awkward buy. That she was as hard as nails seemed to appear in the fact that, thus suddenly bereaved, she was carrying about with her not the slightest indications of grief. But it is not merely the trappings and the suits of woe – Appleby reflected – that are subject to the dictates of fashion, or at least of custom. Banish the widow's bonnet and the widower's arm-band, banish the black-edged writing-paper and envelopes, and at the same time you are likely to see vanish or attenuate themselves the very lineaments of sorrow. One must make no snap judgement on Alice Tytherton's emotional state.

'Colonel Pride, is that a man from a newspaper?' It was at Appleby that Mrs Tytherton was glancing.

'Nothing of the kind.' It clearly cost the Chief Constable an effort not to speak curtly. 'This is Sir John Appleby, whom you may remember I brought over to pay a call, before knowing of this sad event.'

'Yes, of course.' Mrs Tytherton was indifferent. 'How do you do.'

Appleby expressed himself civilly. He had not perhaps the appearance of a man from a newspaper – or at least not of the kind of man from a newspaper who is sent scurrying after a corpse – but he saw no necessity to be offended.

'As a matter of fact,' he said, 'I am another policeman, although a retired one. And the Colonel has asked me to help him. Otherwise, I need hardly say, it would not –'

'What an insipid room.' Thus not very politely cutting Appleby short, Mrs Tytherton looked round her in a kind of slumberous distaste. 'No wonder I seldom enter it. But at least there are cigarettes.' She had pointed to a small glass box on the mantelpiece. 'Please give me one.'

Inspector Henderson obeyed this injunction with a lack of hesitation which told Appleby at once that everything recordable about this room had been recorded. He now took another look at it himself. It was to be supposed that Mrs Tytherton's sense of the insipid stopped short of the Goya, since the character there represented glanced sideways out of his frame with a fiery intensity of regard that was daunting or inspiriting according as to how one cared to receive it. Nor would it quite apply to the only other ancient thing in the room: a Tuscan marriage *cassone* in darkened olive-wood obscurely painted by a *cinquecento* hand with some sacred nuptial occasion. The rest of the furniture was simple enough, and no doubt it could be called insipid or even jejune. Appleby wondered whether the late proprietor of these objects had also been that – or at least whether his wife had so regarded him.

'And there's brandy. I'll have some of that.'

This time, Henderson did hesitate – and to Appleby's sense rather out of delicacy than of professional instinct. On a side-table stood a tray with a decanter, a soda-water syphon, an affair which must have contained ice cubes, and four glasses. Appleby was near enough to see that three of the glasses had been used.

'All right to go ahead, Henderson?' The Chief Constable had moved towards the tray. Perhaps he increasingly disapproved of Mrs Tytherton. But his obedience to a lady's request was automatic.

'Yes, sir. It looks as if some brandy was drunk by two people shortly before the shooting. And after it, of course, by Miss Kentwell. Nothing you could call fingerprints.'

'Somebody rubbed them away, would you say?'

'Possibly so, sir.' Henderson's tone indicated disapproval of such a question in Mrs Tytherton's presence. 'No reason not to use the remaining glass now.' He watched the brandy being poured and handed. 'Can we be of help to you, madam?' he asked formally.

'So far, I have been insufficiently informed. I want to know exactly how my husband died. I am surely entitled to any information you have. Do you, or do you not, yet know who killed him?'

'Inspector Henderson will allow me to reply to that.' Colonel Pride had spoken with surprising promptness. 'Unless your husband killed himself, nobody can declare he *knows* who killed him until a jury has returned a verdict to a judge. The police have to entertain conjectures and suspicions, my dear Mrs Tytherton, but they must not be expected to communicate them even to yourself. Facts are another matter. The Inspector will let you have them at once.'

'Mr Tytherton died – it must have been instantaneously – from a revolver-shot fired at fairly close range into his right temple. He appears to have been sitting at that writing-table in the window, and to have been taken entirely by surprise. He had simply slumped forward where he sat, and there was no sign of a struggle. His death must have occurred shortly before eleven-twenty.'

'And he had been having a drink with somebody?' Mrs Tytherton, her brandy glass at her chin, had taken Henderson's words steadily. 'With somebody unknown?'

'There is that appearance.'

'And he was found by Ronnie – by Mr Ramsden – and that tiresome woman?'

'By Mr Ramsden and Miss Kentwell, madam.'

'If they hadn't come into this room, nothing would have been discovered until today?'

'I have no certain answer to that. It certainly appears true that nobody was alarmed and alerted by the shot, and that none of your guests was aware of anything untoward. Your butler tells me that he would not have made any routine late visit to this room. But perhaps' – Henderson hesitated – 'you would have expected to see Mr Tytherton yourself? He might have visited you to say good night?'

'It was not his habit.'

'Then it does seem probable that, if Mr Ramsden and Miss Kentwell hadn't looked in, your husband's death might not have been discovered till this morning.'

'As it is, you know it happened between his coming

upstairs and twenty past eleven. Even so, anybody in the house might have done it?'

'I really think we ought not at this point—' The Chief Constable had intervened, but Mrs Tytherton cut him short.

'These are still facts. Everybody was scattered, so anybody could have slipped into this room and shot my husband?'

'Yes, madam. That is broadly the present picture.' Henderson paused stonily as Mrs Tytherton drained her glass. 'It may be modified by investigation.'

'And anybody from outside? For instance, Mark Tytherton?'

'We have no present information on Mark Tytherton's movements last night.' Henderson, rather at a loss, did his best with this defensive formula.

'Then the sooner you gather some the better. I have come straight from a totally unexpected interview with him. It appears that he has been staying in the neighbourhood without making the fact known to us.'

'We are aware of the circumstance, madam. Sir John has had a conversation with Mr Mark. With Mr Tytherton, as I ought now to say.'

'You can say what you please.' This meaningless rudeness, Appleby thought, showed Mrs Tytherton as rattled. But then why shouldn't she be? She had lost a husband. She had perhaps acquired, in the person of a step-son, a force to be reckoned with as the new proprietor of Elvedon. 'And please answer my question,' Mrs Tytherton went on. 'Anybody could have come in from outside?'

'Hardly that. Somebody familiar with the place, or who had studied it, or who possessed or had obtained a key to a side door. Security appears to have been reasonable, although not quite what is to be desired in a house containing so much of value as this one.'

'Nothing has been stolen?'

'Nothing that we know of so far. But there may, of course, have been some attempt at robbery, which we have not yet got on the track of. There was, after all, that robbery a couple of years ago. Have you, Madam, any reason to suppose that something of the same sort may have been in question last night?'

'No. And I know very little about the robbery at that time. I was away from home.'

'You mean you were in your London house, Mrs Tytherton?' It was Appleby who asked this.

'I was abroad.'

'For a considerable period?'

'Really, Sir John, I can see no relevance in such a question.'

'The longer you were away, the less specific might be the information about the affair that ever came to you.'

'You think so?' It was clear that Mrs Tytherton judged poorly of this suggestion. 'It was a matter of several months. I was in the South of France, recovering from a serious operation. Can I give you any other information about myself?'

'Thank you, no. But the general pattern of life at Elvedon nowadays must be relevant to our inquiries. You commonly have a small house-party when you are down here?'

'Hardly even a *small* house-party. No more than a few friends. My husband's taste was for very quiet country life.'

'I see. Nothing rackety?'

'Most certainly not.' Mrs Tytherton had adjusted her well-plucked eyebrows to indicate what might have been called aristocratic hauteur.

'But sometimes, perhaps, you have *large* parties for

a weekend – although doubtless of a most decorous sort?'

'Anything of the kind has been quite out of the question. My husband did not care to trouble with a large staff such as is necessary for that sort of thing. Who, for that matter, any longer does?'

'Good thing, too,' Colonel Pride offered. 'Fill your house with mobs of semi-strangers and souse them in inferior champagne. Always was a pretty vulgar notion of life, eh? Few friends quite a different matter.'

'Possibly so.' Here again were observations that Alice Tytherton thought poorly of. 'I was myself brought up to generous notions of hospitality. But the Tythertons have always retained the instincts of the counting-house, Colonel Pride. An eye on the ledger. They dislike even the remotest threat of what is nowadays called getting into the red. They bought Elvedon, but never really expanded to its dimensions. Much of the place is unfurnished to this day, and the kitchens couldn't cater for twenty. It is scarcely the way to take one's place in the county.'

'Can't say I regard ostentation as the best way to stand well with one's neighbours.' Having enunciated this article of simple faith, Colonel Pride suddenly remembered he was conversing with a mourning, even if with an excessively foolish and disagreeable, woman. 'My dear Mrs Tytherton, it was kind of you to come in and renew your offer of help. But we must not tax you further.'

'Catmull says there will be a buffet luncheon at one o'clock.' Mrs Tytherton had put down her empty glass, and stood up. 'I will ask him to avoid any offer of inferior champagne. But Sir John looks as if he might be interested in my late husband's claret.'

'Thank you, but I shall be lunching elsewhere.' Appleby was inclined to react somewhat sharply to insolence. 'And

you must regard me, madam, simply as one of the policemen who will for a little time be around the place.'

'There will be no difficulty about *that*,' Mrs Tytherton
said. And she walked with conscious poise from the room
in which her husband had been murdered.

9

'Interesting woman,' Colonel Pride said dubiously.

'Perhaps so.' Appleby was pacing the room again. 'But I believe I'm more interested in this business of the brandy.' He turned to Henderson. 'How do you arrive at the notion of its having been drunk – apart from Miss Kentwell's swig – almost immediately before Tytherton's death?'

'By treating Miss Kentwell as a reliable witness – which is an act of faith, no doubt. When she came into this room the second time – when she came in and found the body, that is – the tray with the stuff was standing where it stands now. And it hadn't been when she was first here, fifteen minutes or so earlier.'

'Where had it been then?'

'She hadn't noticed it at all.'

'Odd bit of evidence,' Pride said. 'Don't altogether trust it. Seems curious that, in the circumstances, she should have noticed such a thing as a small tray having turned up on an inconspicuous table.'

'Yes, I agree. But it seems that during the few minutes in which she was here on the first occasion she had happened to put her handbag down on that table. Under the shock of discovering the body, she made the same instinctive motion the second time. That is how she came to notice that the tray had appeared there.'

'What does Catmull say about it?' Appleby asked.

'That it usually stands during the evening on the top of

that cupboard in a corner. Tytherton would sometimes shift it elsewhere if he used it.'

'Ramsden?'

'He didn't notice the thing at all, until he looked for it to recruit Miss Kentwell. You say you find the brandy significant, sir?'

'It's only this, Inspector. One doesn't bring a revolver into a room like this on the off-chance of having to defend oneself. One has some positive lethal intention, wouldn't you say? Of course one may intend to kill, or not to kill, the occupant according as to how some attempt at negotiation or the like happens to go. But the probability is that one simply walks in meaning to kill. So what I find hard to envisage is this murderous occasion having as prelude a chummy drink.'

'I see your point, sir. But you're dealing, if I may say so, in no more than likelihood and unlikelihood.'

'Perfectly true. But we ought at least to bear in mind that twenty minutes or thereabouts is an appreciable period of time. Several people could come and go in it.'

'Two visitors rather than one, eh?' The Chief Constable nodded wisely. 'Perfectly feasible thing. And plenty of people around who might have dropped in on the chap innocently enough. Which reminds me, Henderson. About time we had them formally on parade, wouldn't you say?'

'Yes, sir.' Henderson looked at his watch. 'It's true I've had only sketchy statements from some of them so far. And at least one of them is already impatient to get away. Mr Carter.'

'And just who,' Appleby asked, 'is Mr Carter?'

'I don't know what the fellow does.' It was Pride who produced this. 'Except, it seems, hang around Alice Tytherton. Or that, my dear John, is the gossip. Rather a raffish crowd, you know. One keeps on coming back to that.'

'Does one?' Appleby was amused. 'As far as a motive for this crime goes, I'd call it an area we still have to explore. *Carter, enamoured of Mrs Tytherton,* as an old play might say. What about somebody called Mrs Graves – whom our friend Raffaello was badgering? Is she *Mrs Graves, enamoured of Tytherton?*'

'I think we can safely say some relationship exists, but you can judge for yourself after lunch, John. We'll have the whole crowd lined up, and invite them to say anything they want to, eh? Not forgetting the missing heir from his local pub.'

'Whom I'll make myself responsible for contacting.' Appleby moved to the door. 'And now, do you and the Inspector go and sample that woman's damned claret. I'm taking a country walk.'

'Henderson and I intend to drink water, and in a room by ourselves. That right, Inspector?'

'Decidedly, sir. We're both on duty, after all. And I rather think Sir John must be reckoned so too.'

'Quite right.' The Chief Constable chuckled. 'Appreciate your attitude very much, my dear Henderson. Get this nasty thing cleared up as soon as possible. Eh, John?'

'Well, yes. By dinner-time, perhaps. Certainly before we go to bed.'

'Sir?' There was a startled note in Henderson's voice. 'Don't you feel that this may be – well, rather a complicated case?'

'Oh, decidedly. And that's the hopeful thing, Inspector. Plenty to worry at, and so elucidate at a tolerable pace. It's the really simple affairs that can be a month's hard work. Shall I tell Mark Tytherton it's two o'clock for your next session?'

*

The vicarage lay beyond the kitchen gardens, the church beyond the vicarage, and the village beyond the church. It was thus that Appleby, proposing to seek refreshment and perhaps information in the local pub, found himself viewing the Reverend Mr Voysey in his garden. Mr Voysey sat within the shade of a rustic arbour, in front of him a table decorously spread with a snowy linen cloth, and on the cloth a generous provision of bread, cheese, cold ham, apples, and a jug of what was perhaps cider. Appleby, passing on the other side of a hedge, would not have paused before this spectacle of Sabine plenty had he not been hailed by the person in innocent enjoyment of it. Mr Voysey had raised an arm in a gesture combining arrestment with the muted suggestion of ecclesiastical blessing.

'Ah, Sir John! Whither away so fast? Will you not enter and lunch with me? Capital Double Gloucester, and very tolerable Beauties of Bath. Or ought one to say Beauty of Baths? Do you go in for apples?'

'Yes, indeed. They take the place with me of poor Sherlock Holmes's bees. But I must resist your invitation. I rather hope for what they call a working lunch in your village inn.'

'The Hanged Man. A curious name for a convivial resort. The English had a developed taste for the macabre long before the invention of Sunday newspapers. How does it go with the kettle of fish at the big house?'

'Not yet quite on the boil. May I ask you something?'

'By all means. But pray step through the wicket. Village life, as you must know, is divided between the twin activities of peeping and eavesdropping.' Voysey waited until Appleby had obeyed this prudent injunction and sat down on a bench beside him. 'Of course you must not ask me for the secrets of the confessional. None are available. Once, as a curate, I had to work in a parish where that kind of thing went on. Confessions, I mean. Not, it seemed, the sort of things that it would have been at all interesting to hear confessed.'

'Mr Voysey, it has occurred to me to wonder whether, at our encounter earlier this morning, you told me quite everything that you might have done.'

'Ah – about the Elvedon folk in general. Perhaps you are right. I hinted disapprobation, and failed to document it. I might have been motivated by no more than the fact that they don't much come to church. No more they do. And where a parish includes a landowner in a large squirarchal way, the parson does appreciate his giving some thought to what used to be called the public discharge of his religious duties. However, Sir John, times change. And it's not what those people fail to do in public that I deprecate. It's what they don't bother to keep private. One doesn't care to report evil of a man one will presently be reading the burial service over, and that must excuse part of my reticence. Tytherton had a mistress called Mrs Graves – Cynthia Graves. She was always around the place, and in fact is there now, as you probably know. I don't know whether adultery becomes yet more sinful when carried out under one's wife's roof. I'd have to ask the Bishop.' Mr Voysey selected an apple as he offered this clerical jest. 'But it certainly becomes more blackguardly. And they have taken no care to conceal it. Their servants have known, and so the village has known. Which is something that's bad for morality at large.'

'And Mrs Tytherton has been standing for this?'

'Mrs Tytherton may not have been in a strong position to protest. Something like open scandal there too, I'm sorry to say. But *that* side of the thing I think I'll let you find out for yourself.'

'Thank you; I have a notion it won't be difficult.' Appleby paused. 'As a matter of fact, it wasn't about the sexual ethos of Elvedon that I was thinking, although I'm most grateful for what you have told me. It was about the young Tytherton – Mark.'

'But, my dear Sir John, it was about spotting Mark two days ago in the park that I took particular occasion to speak to you.'

'That is true. But I had a sense – it's something my curious profession has much refined in me, you know – that there was something you *hadn't* spoken about.'

'And so there was.' For some moments Mr Voysey concentrated upon removing the skin from his apple in a single spiral paring. 'I reported a certainty, and suppressed a conjecture. Or, perhaps, less a conjecture than a fancy. And the trouble is that I can no longer be confident as to when it actually visited me. Are you interested in badgers?'

'Uncommonly.' Appleby appeared quite unsurprised by this question. 'We have several setts in our wood at Dream. My wife and I both put in a good deal of time watching them.'

'Then you know that last night would have been ideal for the purpose. A very light wind, and an excellent moon. I went badger-watching myself. Perhaps I may be allowed to mention that I have contributed one or two observations on the creatures to the journals – as an unassuming field-naturalist, you will understand.'

'I must get hold of them,' Appleby said politely.

'I should also mention that I obey a certain instinct of privacy when pursuing this necessarily nocturnal vocation. A night-prowling parson is regarded with suspicion in the countryside. Evil motives are imputed to him. I have sometimes thought that this must stem from the just ill-repute of certain of the Pre-Reformation clergy. You will recall that "limitours and othere holy freres" are described by Chaucer as frequently up to no good in their wanderings.'

'Most interesting,' Appleby said. He saw that Mr Voysey was not to be hurried.

'As it happened, the earlier part of my vigil went un-rewarded. It was in a patch of the woodland where there is an ash-association with a ground flora of bluebells and dog's mercury as co-dominants. I had great hopes of it. However, nothing turned up, and I recalled another site where I had promised myself a long period of observation. This was in a bramble thicket beyond the other side of the park. I would be delighted to show it to you. One very large bush has been curiously hollowed out, and I have a strong suspicion that the badgers use it as a sleeping-out place. Successful observations of these have not been common. As I walked, my mind was intent upon its possibilities.'

'But you observed something else, all the same?'

'Precisely. The figure of a man, hurrying across the park from the direction of Elvedon itself. I withdrew into shadow before, I believe, he became aware of me. He was more likely, I judged, to be a poacher than a harmless fellow naturalist. However he was almost certain to be one of my parishioners, and a meeting might well have been embarrassing.'

'But he turned out' – and Appleby looked hard at the Reverend Mr Voysey – 'to be young Mark Tytherton again, after all?'

'That is precisely what I cannot say.'

'This time, you didn't see his face?'

'I don't *think* I did. Certainly I was less aware of his face than of his *pace*. He was walking very rapidly, and with more than a suggestion of agitation.'

'At what time was this?'

'At a guess, round about half-past eleven. But I could by no means be confident to within thirty minutes or so.'

'Mr Voysey, you are now giving me information which

may be of the utmost seriousness. You must try to clarify your impressions. Here is a man walking rapidly across parkland on a moonlight night. You don't see his features, but you speak of "a suggestion of agitation". Can you say just how that suggestion conveyed itself to you?'

'This is most perplexing. I really don't think I can.'

'Was he making gestures?'

'Gestures? I think not. No – positively not.'

'Was his haste such that he appeared to be in danger of stumbling?'

'That may well have been so.' Mr Voysey had brightened. 'Yes, I believe his progress might justly be so described.'

'Did he, while within your observation, look behind him?'

'As if he were being pursued? I think it very likely that he did. In the circumstances, that is to say.'

'But we know nothing about his circumstances. If he was a poacher, would you have expected to notice him as carrying something? *Was* he carrying anything?'

'Sir John, you must stop. Every question you ask merely serves to distort the very vague image of the occasion that I actually possess. Can you understand that?'

'Most certainly I can, so let me stop building up a fancy picture for you. I shall not even ask you to estimate how close you came to this man. But one point perhaps we can get clear – and it is really a vital one. Just when did the name "Mark Tytherton", or the thought "Mark again", or anything of the kind, first come into your head?'

'I don't know.' Mr Voysey had put down his apple-core on the plate before him, and was regarding Appleby soberly. 'That, my dear sir, is the answer I must give you, however much it makes me appear a fool. Was it a thought synchronous with my actual observation of this figure? Or was it something that came to me retrospectively, when they rang me up from Elvedon this morning, and told me what had happened? I cannot return a confident answer – such as I can, for example, about my previous daylight encounter with the young man not far from the same spot. So I am a very bad witness, I fear.'

'My dear Mr Voysey, the human memory is a very odd contraption, and you have an instinct to respect its oddity. I believe that, as a witness, you might get rather a high mark from a judge.'

'It is a test, I confess, that I have no eagerness to face.'

'Giving evidence in a criminal trial?' Appleby rose from the bench on which he had been sitting during this curious conversation. 'Far be it from me to be needlessly depressing. But I fear it is extremely improbable that you will not find yourself so engaged before the year is out.'

10

The Hanged Man proved to be a hostelry of small preten-
sion, although its saloon bar seemed to do a certain amount
of trade of the gin-and-tonic, chicken-sandwich order with
passing motorists. Appleby avoided this unpromising ter-
rain, only to find that the public bar was at this time of day
attracting no custom at all. But the fact didn't appear to
make his own arrival the more welcome; it was from an unresponsive character, whose bearing hinted a sense of something demeaning in attending to so inconsiderable an order,
that he succeeded in extracting a pint of bitter and a plate
of bread and cheese. The suggestion that it was a fine day
got no response whatever; the further and more expansive
assertion that it was a very nice countryside round about
here elicited no more than a melancholic sigh. So Appleby
resigned himself to solitary reflection. It might be quite a
useful exercise.

So far, there were two strands visible in this affair, and
they were not of a sort to come together readily into a pattern. In the first of these strands he was himself, it might be
said, a tenuous thread. A couple of years ago there had been
some not very spectacular art theft at Elvedon; quite recently the deprived owner, Maurice Tytherton, had taken it
into his head that he would like to make the acquaintance of
Sir John Appleby, a celebrated authority on such matters;
the said Sir John had presented himself at Elvedon (this as a
consequence of a rather childish stratagem on the part of

Colonel Pride) to find that Tytherton had just met a violent end – and to find, too, that an old adversary of his, the not too reputable art-dealer Egon Raffaello, had been staying there as the dead man's guest. All this might, or might not, add up; and it was certainly desirable to obtain much more specific information about the theft that stood at the beginning of the series.

What had tended to obscure this strand in the affair, and to obtrude the other, was really what might be called the moralism of Tommy Pride. Pride had a bad conscience about not having been quite frank about the occasion of his taking Appleby over to Elvedon, and this was sharpened by his perhaps obsessive sense that the place was a haunt of vice. Or at least that it was full of people who exhibited the most rotten bad form – as Tytherton had done, most strikingly, by bringing his mistress into his wife's house. But at least it seemed true that there *was* this strand to the mystery; that the house-party at Elvedon – not to speak of the expatriate son, quartered in this pub, and either seen or not seen at a compromising time of night by Mr Voysey when looking for badgers – did hint a state of affairs which might generate some species of *crime passionnel*.

Brooding over this, there suddenly came into Appleby's head the totally incongruous figure of Miss Jane Kentwell, celebrated as having found the body. *Que diable allait-elle faire dans cette galère?* She had very little appearance of being likely to find herself at home in raffish society, any more than she had of connoisseurship in the arts. Perhaps she really did make something of a profession as a seeker out of charitable gifts and bequests – but had she been admitted to Elvedon on that ticket? One had no sense of it as a place in which any philanthropic bounty was likely at all notably to flow. There was a small note of the enigmatic, Appleby told himself, about Miss Kentwell.

It was at this point in his meditation that Appleby noticed he was no longer alone in the public bar of the Hanged Man. A person of superior appearance had entered, been provided with a tankard, and modestly retreated to an unobtrusive corner. Appleby took another look at this superior person, and saw that he was none other than Catmull the butler.

There is no prescribed etiquette for casual rencontre between butlers and retired Commissioners of Police. The thing has to be played by ear. Appleby's manner of coping now was dictated by a lively sense of something interesting that must lurk in Catmull's having made a break from Elvedon at the present hour. The man had either served his buffet luncheon and immediately downed tools, or deputed the whole operation to some subordinate menial. Perhaps like Appleby himself he had felt a strong compulsion to withdraw and think matters out. Reflecting thus, Appleby risked an intrusive move. He picked up his own tankard and crossed over to Catmull's corner.

'May I join you?' he asked. 'It seems pretty quiet here today.'

Catmull nodded. The gesture indicated at once that when he stepped outside the Elvedon ring-fence it was into a position of equality with all men. Appleby approved of this, although he wasn't sure that he approved of Catmull. And if Catmull was startled by being accosted by the Chief Constable's companion he gave no sign of it.

'It's quiet now,' he said, 'and that's why I came here. But you wait. The reporters are on their way now, aren't they? And this is where they'll put up.'

'I don't doubt it, Mr Catmull. And you'll have hard work keeping them out of Elvedon itself.'

'That's a true word. Mere trippers too there'll be, once

the radio and the telly and the evening papers have come out with it. No lack of drinkers in the Hanged Man tonight.' Catmull paused. 'Queer that you and the Colonel should come asking for Mr Tytherton like that.'

'An odd coincidence, certainly.'

'Hadn't been at Elvedon before, I think?'

'Never. Colonel Pride was to introduce me to your late employer. I have an idea that Mr Tytherton wanted to have a talk about the pictures he lost a couple of years ago.'

'Ah, now that goes with what Mrs Catmull says!' Catmull was momentarily looking at Appleby through narrowed eyes. 'Interesting, that is.'

'And what does Mrs Catmull say? I don't quite follow you.'

' "Why, that's him that was in my book," she said. When I told her your name not an hour ago, sir. "That's him I read about," Mrs Catmull said. But by a book she doesn't of course *mean* a book. Mrs Catmull isn't highly educated. She calls a magazine a book, sir – like most women do.' Catmull seemed here to touch on a misogynistic note. 'Intending, you see, that she'd read about Sir John Appleby as one going after thieved pictures, and the like.'

'It was certainly an interest of mine at one time, Mr Catmull.'

'Well, here are you coming to talk to Mr Tytherton about such things today, and here is Mr Tytherton getting himself shot dead last night. If you ask me, it deserves thinking about, that does.' Catmull paused. 'That Mr Raffaello, now. Never been to Elvedon before in my time, he hasn't. And he's another one, it seems, that has to do with pictures and statues and the like. Snoops around them, too, in a way I don't half like. Peering into places, like a guest who is anything of a gentleman shouldn't. An eye should be kept on him, to my mind. Given his marching orders, he ought to

82

be.' Catmull's tone had suddenly turned almost vicious. 'But who's to do that? Who does the bloody place belong to now. I'd like to know? But those in service aren't told such things. Mrs Tytherton, she'll go off now with you know who to France. And Mrs Catmull and me – well, a month's wages handed us by a lawyer, it's likely to be – and my good man pack your bag.'

'I have no doubt that Mrs Catmull and yourself would readily find a suitably superior new situation.' Appleby had listened to the butler's sudden outburst with some curiosity. 'But it seems possible that young Mr Tytherton, who is said to have returned to England, may propose to keep up Elvedon in the same style as his father.'

'Back in England – him?' If Catmull wasn't genuinely startled, Appleby thought, he was an uncommonly good actor. 'Much good he'll do us.' He stared morosely into what was now evidently an empty tankard. 'In fact, damn-all.'

'Would you care for another pint, Mr Catmull?'

'Well, sir, I don't mind if I do.' Catmull's glance as he said this didn't match with his casual tone. There was a curious hint of masked calculation in it. He is a man – Appleby told himself as he took both tankards to the bar – thoroughly pleased with his own cunning.

But when he returned with the beer there was surely nothing but stupidity on Catmull's face as he doggedly pursued his aggrieved note.

'Of course we have a bit put by – Mrs Catmull and me. Years in good service, we've seen, and careful living all the time. So there's a small nest-egg, I don't deny. But no possessions, sir. Scarcely a stick to set up with, if that's what it comes to. And the price of so much as a kitchen chair something chronic today. Just what I have in my pantry at the big house, sir. Nothing else at all. Just everything there. Came to me from my father, they did. No class about them. And nothing else. Not so much as our own bed to comfort one another in.' A long pull at his fresh pint had perhaps prompted this last affecting thought. 'Time was, sir, when folk in the position of Mrs C. and me could set up with rooms for single gentlemen. Chambers, one could call them, and charge accordingly. Prohibitive now. Absolutely prohibitive.'

'I have no doubt the capital expenditure would be considerable.' Appleby, although unable to feel any keen sympathy for the conjectured economic plight of the Catmulls, said what he could. 'Haven't you regularly been left in sole charge of Elvedon while Mr and Mrs Tytherton had been in London, or abroad?'

'Oh, decidedly, sir. Except for Mr Ramsden as often as not, and young Mr Archie Tytherton the nephew from time to time, we take full charge, sir. Every confidence has been reposed in us.'

'I'm very glad to hear it. When there is to be some radical change of plan for a big house, upper servants are frequently left in residence as caretakers over an indefinite period. On suitable board wages, of course. You must be aware of that. If it happens at Elvedon, it will give you time to look around.'

'That's very true, sir – very true, indeed.' The glint of cunning had returned to Catmull's face. His manner, moreover, was shading into what might be called the professional-servile. 'And I should be most grateful if any good word to that effect could be said, Sir John. Any influential word – from one of high standing such as yourself.'

'I am most unlikely to be consulted.'

'It has always been a great responsibility. The house contains so much that is valuable – quite apart from the pictures, even. But speaking of them, sir, might I ask if that Mr Raffaello – we were having a word about him a moment ago, sir – makes a business of buying such things and selling them again?'

'Yes, he does.'

'And perhaps, Sir John, it wouldn't always be quite above the board? A shady one, he seems to me.'

'I am afraid I can say nothing whatever about that.'

'Well, sir, I think I'd call that a significant reply. And in London, I imagine, there would be plenty others of the same sort?'

'If you mean dealers who are not very scrupulous about the authenticity of what they sell, or careful to establish the seller's just title, that is certainly so. But you must not suppose me to be suggesting anything of the sort about Mr Raffaello or anybody else.'

'But you would have had dealings with such in your time?'

'Dealings with them? I've seen some of them into gaol, if that's what you mean.'

'And perhaps they would continue in their wickedness, sir, when they came out again? A sad thought.'

'It's certainly true of some of them.'

'Their names would be in the papers – at the time, I mean, of their being convicted?'

'Dear me, yes. You could look them up.' The cunning of Catmull, Appleby was reflecting, seemed of a somewhat primitive order. He was surely a singularly unsuitable person to leave in charge of a large house filled with valuable objects. 'But they have to be very clever indeed, I may say, not to get pretty quickly caught out. The ownership of most works of art of outstanding value is common knowledge nowadays. It's all recorded in catalogues and so on. So it isn't possible to buy, say, a Goya which you know to be stolen and stick it happily above your diningroom mantel-piece. All you could do would be to lock it up, and some-times go and gloat over it in private. There are people prepared to spend big money buying themselves such a pleasure – but they are few, and singularly hard to find.' Appleby finished his second pint – thus conscientiously con-sumed in the interest of detective investigation – and pushed away the tankard. 'In fact, Mr Catmull, important works of art are about the last wares to which I could conscientiously recommend a would-be thief to turn his attention.'

'Most interesting, sir. May I ask what, in fact, you would positively recommend?'

'My dear Mr Catmull, that would be telling.'

11

Catmull didn't press his hopeful inquiry; instead, he consulted his watch, got to his feet, offered Appleby a modified form of professional bow, and withdrew with dignity from the Hanged Man. The cares of Elvedon were gathering once more around him.

Appleby recalled that he had undertaken to contact Mark Tytherton. It looked as if, immediately after their last meeting in the presence of the unspeakable Raffaello and the enigmatically philanthropical Miss Kentwell, the young man had made his way into the further presence of his stepmother – and perhaps, briefly, into that of his dead father before the ambulance had received him. Alice Tytherton's manner had not suggested that this occasion of mutual condolence – which in conditions of any sort of decency ought to have been a moving one – had brought her any comfort or consolation whatever. The widow hadn't, in fact, so much as pretended to grief. As for Mark, he had been upon the occasion of his encounters with Appleby, Raffaello, and Miss Kentwell at least in a discernible state of shock. It might of course be shock over something done and not merely over something heard or suffered. That was an open question. That it should remain an open question, at least for the time, appeared to have been Mr Voysey's anxiety – an anxiety which had partly explained itself from the vicar's confusion, psychologically persuasive enough, as to just what had come into his head when. Voysey – when, as it were, going by the book – didn't care for Mark Tytherton at all. Mark was a young man of irregular life, at odds with his family, and not at all disposed to exhibit those professions and attitudes upon which it is comforting to be able to rely in a Christian and a gentleman. But an unregenerate Voysey – conceivably a wise and humane Voysey – would acknowledge at a pinch a soft spot for the wandering heir. Appleby wasn't confident that he didn't harbour such a soft spot himself. But soft spots, while becoming in a clergyman, are wholly undesirable in a policeman. Appleby's business was to find Mark again – and perhaps to twist his tail a little before introducing him into the society of the Chief Constable and Inspector Henderson.

One must suppose Mark to have found Elvedon unwelcoming. It was improbable that he didn't now own the place. Outcast heirs commonly discover themselves to be heirs after all. But he seemed not to have announced himself as at all settling in. If he hadn't departed altogether, which was something that common prudence would surely counterindicate, he had presumably returned to this wretched pub. There was a probability that he was somewhere lurking in it now. Appleby resolved to investigate. He got to his feet and walked over to the bar. A detached observer might have remarked in him a somewhat ominous gathering of authority as he moved. The taciturn and discontented publican, who was disdainfully puddling glasses in an invisible sink of what was doubtless dirty water, glanced at him with a new wariness as he approached.

'I think,' Appleby said, 'that you have a few rooms here? There is a gentleman staying with you now?'

'Yes, there is.'

'You know who he happens to be?'

'I don't know much about the folk in these parts. I haven't been here long.'

'Why should you suppose him to belong to these parts? I suppose he just drove up, didn't he, like anyone else motoring around?'

'He drove up, all right – in a taxi from the junction. He's no business of mine.'

'But you know now who he is?'

'Well, one of my regulars has said something. I didn't much attend to it.' Momentarily, the publican showed signs of fight. 'And who are you, anyway?'

'I am Sir John Appleby.'

'Never heard of you.'

'There is no reason why you should have. I advise you to answer my questions, all the same. You have heard what has happened at Elvedon Court?'

'Everybody has heard that. The police are there. I don't want any trouble.'

'There is no reason to suppose you are going to meet any.' Appleby wondered what inconsiderable irregularities in the conduct of the Hanged Man were the occasion of this defensive attitude. 'Where is this gentleman now?'

'I don't know. In his room, perhaps.'

'Be so good as to tell him I want to speak to him.'

'There's a woman with him.'

'That is quite irrelevant.' Appleby dissimulated his surprise at this blurted out information. 'You mean that he arrived with a woman?'

'Nothing of the kind. She came asking for him – just before you came in. One of the nobs from the big house, I'd say. Dressed up to the nines. I sent her up. Number Two. There's only Number One and Number Two here. No class, this place. Not much trade, either.'

'Thank you. You needn't trouble yourself further. It doesn't sound as if Number Two will be hard to find. I hope you're washing those glasses in running water.'

And Appleby left the public bar. This mild police bullying, he reflected, came back to him quite naturally from long, long ago.

The little staircase was dirty. There was a shabby landing and a small corridor. There were voices, raised voices, from behind the second door he came to. He had never found keyholes attractive. They were even less attractive than bullying. He knocked briskly at the door and walked in.

'Who the hell are you?' Young Mark Tytherton, standing in the middle of the small ugly room, had swung round furiously. He had a trick of reacting to stimuli in an over-violent way.

'You know who I am. Appleby. Introduce me, please.'

'This is Mrs Graves. Please take her away and bury her.'

To a witticism so logically bizarre as this it is not easy to frame a reply, and for a moment Appleby found himself looking speechlessly at the lady – almost, indeed, like an undertaker making a rapid calculation of the dimensions of a corpse. Not that there was anything corpse-like about Mrs Graves; she seemed as alive as an electric eel, and no more comfortable for the purpose of making passes at. But tastes of course differ, and those of an elderly policeman are not of an exotic sort. It was possible that this snaky slinky person was precisely Mark Tytherton's style – as she was reputed to have been that of his late father. Perhaps – extremely unedifying as the thought was – the occasion of this prodigal son's home-coming had been a rumour of the attractiveness of his father's mistress. She couldn't be thought of as a fatted calf, indeed; rather she would pass very well as a serpent of old Nile. And perhaps the not very gallant injunction that Appleby had just received was a consequence of no more than a lovers' quarrel. Not that they looked like lovers – even lovers who had fallen out. They had been confronting each other, absurdly, from either side of an iron bedstead which showed no sign of having had to resign itself to illicit amorous purposes. And they presented as convincing an appearance of mortal enemies as Appleby could remember ever having seen together in a room.

'I don't in the least want to take either of you away,' Appleby said. 'Nor even to interrupt a private social occasion. What I have to tell you is that the police resume their investigation at Elvedon at two o'clock, and would be obliged if you could be available to them then.'

'This fellow follows me around, talking like a coppers' manual.' Mark Tytherton offered this observation to Mrs Graves in what was momentarily almost a conciliatory tone. 'It's your turn now, woman. Talk to him. Chat him up. I'm going down to get a drink. I'll need it, if I'm to be put through some third degree.'

'If you choose, Mr Tytherton, you need say nothing at all to anyone until you have taken legal advice. And that, madam, applies to you as well. But if I might myself have a word with both of you now, the later stage of the affair might be simplified.'

'And what the hell do you mean by that?' Mark Tytherton demanded.

'Only what I say. And I assure you that I am a totally disinterested observer of this affair. It is a complicated affair. Also an onion of an affair, one might say, requiring a good deal of stripping.'

'No need to be coarse,' Mrs Graves said haughtily. 'And I don't understand your position at all. It seems quite irregular.'

'So it is, madam. I may be called a Baker Street Irregular. As for my coarseness, there is perhaps rather a lot of it around. It's my idea that a certain amount of it can conceivably be got out of the way in not too public a fashion. But I warn you that I may be wrong.'

'There may be something in that!' Mark Tytherton came out with this vehemently. 'It's the absolute damned indecency of these salt bitches that really gets me down. It dragged *him* down.'

'Mr Tytherton, I have already listened to a certain amount of your intemperate speech. If you want my help –'

'A snooping copper's *help*?'

'Yes – my help. If you want it, you'll employ the language of a gentleman.'

'Creeping Christ! The man's out of Noah's Ark.'

'Then moderate your tongue, or back into the Ark I go. Leaving you, incidentally, in not too agreeable a position. What were you doing, prowling around Elvedon not far short of midnight last night?'

'What was I doing last night, out in the pale moonlight?' Mark produced this snatch of music-hall melody defiantly enough, but he had gone pale nevertheless. So, for that matter, had Mrs Graves. Perhaps, Appleby thought, these two, despite their present enmity, had been playing Romeo and Juliet under the same resplendent moon which had enabled Miss Kentwell and the attendant Ramsden to survey the countryside from the leads of Elvedon. Or perhaps they had been quite otherwise employed. They were certainly exchanging a glance quite as much of complicity as enmity now. 'What was I doing?' Mark repeated. 'Nothing that I see any reason to tell you about.'

'That is a perfectly legitimate reply. But it means that you *were* on the prowl?'

'Who wouldn't be on a fine night, if the alternative was skulking in this bloody pub?'

'I take the point. But the skulking was your own idea,

after all. If you had driven straight to Elvedon, I don't know just how lovingly or civilly you would have been received. But I have no reason to suppose you'd have been turned away from the place.'

'Do you suppose I'd have wanted to spend a night under the same roof as those two –' With an enormous effort, Mark checked himself. 'With those two gentlewomen?'

'He's a straight nut-case,' Mrs Graves offered unexpectedly. 'He has a thing about his mother.'

Appleby glanced at this disagreeable and far from nicely bred woman with a certain respect. She had at least said something that she believed to be true; something that was conceivably a firm stepping-stone in a thoroughly boggy affair. What Mark had earlier represented in himself as a loss of nerve and lack of guts – the reason, he had maintained, of his not going straight to Elvedon upon his arrival in England – had quite possibly its real occasion in what Mrs Graves vulgarly called a thing about his mother. Appleby had heard nothing about the first Mrs Tytherton; about how far back, so to speak, she lay either in her husband's life or her son's. She might be dead, or she might be alive and divorced. She might have been a faithless wife to Tytherton. Or Tytherton might have been a faithless husband to her, as he appeared to have been to his second wife, Alice Tytherton. There was plenty of room for conjecture. There was also a need for simple information, if anything was to be made of this new dimension of the affair. Mark Tytherton himself could supply much of it, and Appleby wasn't sure that, only a few minutes before, the young man hadn't betrayed a certain willingness to parley. The presence of Mrs Graves, however, was unlikely to facilitate the process. And Mrs Graves, although no doubt harbouring mysteries of her own, would keep. It would be a good idea to get rid of her. Having determined on this, Appleby made a sudden move over to the window, and glanced out.

'Ah!' he said. 'I thought I heard a car. But not yet. However, they'll be here at any time now.'

'The police?' Mrs Graves asked sharply.

'I think not. The Hanged Man doesn't interest the police at the moment. I mean the press. Reporters and photographers, madam. This is certainly where they will put up. I'm surprised they're not here already.'

'Photographers?'

'Oh, most certainly, madam. You will all be on the front page of the dailies tomorrow.' Appleby looked at Mrs Graves appraisingly. 'It's a pity you're not looking quite your best. At least, I suppose that's so, for you're certainly not looking too good. Mr Tytherton, you agree?'

'I wouldn't care to be ungallant,' Mark said with a vicious grin. 'But, since you ask me, I'm bound to say she looks like the cat's breakfast.'

'You cads!' Mrs Graves said. But although she had produced this antique locution with all the splendour of a lady in a Somerset Maugham play, she was grabbing her bag and making for the door.

'Don't be bullied by them,' Appleby said kindly. 'Take your time over the necessary repairs, and insist on pleasing yourself as to how you pose. I'd suggest as background the loggia on Elvedon's west front. More dignified than being caught in a pot house.'

But Mrs Graves was gone.

'She was quite right,' Mark said. '*You* can't be a gentleman either.' For a moment he looked almost cheerful. 'Why did you get rid of her? What do you want to know?'

'Eventually, I want to know everything about your

movements over the last twenty-four hours. But that's something you may want to think about.'

'Why should I want to think about it? In order to make up a pack of lies?'

'Not necessarily that at all. For instance, there may be other people whose interests you have to consider. And as for the question I fired at you about being in the park late last night, I'll tell you the basis of that at once. It's simply the vicar again. He was out looking for badgers, and he's not sure he didn't see you instead. But he'd be very far from swearing to it, if put in a witness-box. You can be confident of that.'

'What a damned odd thing for you to tell me.' Mark stared at Appleby, genuinely perplexed. 'Well, he *did* see me. For that matter, I saw him.'

'You visited Elvedon?'

'Take it easy, Appleby. You've got me in the park at midnight. One step at a time.' As he produced this frivolous response the young man made a weary gesture and sat down on the bed, which creaked dismally beneath him. 'Or try something else.'

'I very much want to try something else – on a different time-scale, as it were. When did your father's second marriage take place?'

'Fourteen years ago – when I was fourteen.'

'Your mother was dead?'

'No, she died some years later. There had been a divorce.'

'It worried you?'

'When you're not talking out of that bobby's guide it's only to take a turn as a child-guidance officer. Of course it worried me.'

'And continued to – to an extent justifying what that beastly woman said: that you have a thing about your mother?'

'I can't think why I don't knock you down.' Mark Tytherton remained unbelligerently on the bed. 'But I see your picture. And it's really fair enough.' He frowned. 'The thing's not an obsession,' he said, 'even if it has more or less occasioned the way I live. I'm not a nut-case, despite what that cheap little tart said.' His expression darkened. 'I won't plead diminished responsibility, or any crap like that.'

'The divorce was an unfortunate one?'

'It was all pretty filthy. And one of those affairs in which the judge feels he has to talk a lot of the muck into the published record. I was in my first year at public school.'

'I see. But all this is very much past history, Mr Tytherton. Have you lately been disturbed by some sense of that history in a fashion repeating itself?'

'What should put that in your head: my father ditching Alice as he ditched my mother – and this time in favour of a mere whore?'

'It's conceivable. And may I ask another child-guidance question? Have you felt a very keen antagonism towards your father?'

'Not for years.' Mark produced this with a promptness at which he himself appeared surprised. 'I used to want to kill him. But everything changes with the years – even these fearfully deep things. Passions wear themselves away. It's pretty terrifying, really. There's a French chap who wrote a dozen books on that. I once read them when I was ill.'

'He wrote them when *he* was ill.' Appleby would not have thought of Mark Tytherton as a likely amateur of Marcel Proust. 'But other passions crop up.'

'Oh, quite. Trifling and peripheral things' – Mark's vocabulary was changing as he talked – 'that take on a sudden symbolical significance. I cared, you see, that my father's life should be degraded by a series of rotten women. It seemed a shame. He wasn't a bad sort. And it's such a revolting sight: a man old enough to know better, help-less before that silly tickling, and being dragged about by the nose, or rather the –'

'Quite so. But you didn't return to England, Mr Tyther-ton, to act as an elevating influence, struggle with your father for his immortal soul, and redeem Elvedon from its degraded condition as a haunt of vice?'

'You can also talk bloody tough. And of course I didn't come back with any kid's notions of the sort. When I was very small –' Mark hesitated. *'Listen,'* he said oddly. 'For here's the beans.'

'I am listening.'

'When I was very small, and my mother was getting dressed to go out to dinner or something, I used to be allowed to get the jewel-cases from a small safe in her bedroom. A fascinating hiding-place, you see. Absolute magic in it.'

'Yes, indeed.'

'And then the jewels themselves!' Mark pulled himself up. 'Let's just say they were of very considerable value indeed. And, incidentally, they were her own. Emotionally, that's not a great point with me. I mean that the legal posi-tion isn't such a point. The things just were, quite obviously to me, my mother's. Part of her.'

'And it is these trinkets that crop up with what you call a sudden symbolical significance?'

'Yes. And at least you understand what I'm talking about.'

'And where are they now?'

'That woman has them. The trollop you've just sent packing from this room.'

'Can you be sure of that?'

'Of course I can. It stands to reason. And I had a go at her this morning as I came away from Elvedon.' Mark was becoming excited. 'I ran into her – and took the opportunity of telling her I thought of wringing her ruddy neck.'

'My dear young man!'

'It paid off. At least it panicked her. She came to this pub to tell me a pack of lies about *not* having them. But one doesn't believe a harlot on a thing like that.'

'I see.' Appleby looked at Mark soberly. 'And now I think that you and I had better get back to Elvedon.'

'I'm damned if I –'

'Don't be a fool. You're in a fix, and you know it. You've told me quite a lot, and I believe you. But you have more to tell. Think it over, please, as we walk across the park. If I can honestly help you, I will. But being a good deal franker than you have been so far is your best chance of scrambling out of trouble.'

12

The walk accomplished itself in complete silence until the two men stood at the bottom of the steps leading up to the main portico of Elvedon. At the top, side by side with the sentinel-like constable who was doubtless preparing himself to salute, stood Colonel Pride. He was clearly waiting for Appleby, and expecting him to appear upon his hour. And this was happening, since the stable clock now struck twice.

'Who's that?' There was a sharp note in Mark Tytherton's voice, and he had come to a halt.

'The Chief Constable. I'll introduce you, and he will take you to an officer called Inspector Henderson. Henderson will take down, and ask you to sign, any statement you may care to make.'

'So this is it. I could send for the family lawyer – that sort of thing?'

'Most definitely. Indeed, the police are often inclined to prefer it that way.'

'They must put up with me *solus*.' Mark Tytherton's chin had gone up. 'Only – do you know? – there's just one thing I'd like to tell you yourself, here and now. Steady me a bit, perhaps. Or call it burning a boat, if you like. It's true I was here last night.'

'Thank you. Now up we go.'

They climbed. Pride watched them impassively, his hands behind his back. They might have been holding a pair of handcuffs.

'Tommy, this is Mr Tytherton. Colonel Pride.'

'How do you do?' Pride shook hands instantly. 'Let me condole with you, sir. Where's your bag?'

'Thank you.' Mark Tytherton was taken aback. 'My bag?'

'This is an unbecoming business, sir. Putting up in the inn. Your relations with your step-mother may not be good. But you ought now to be under this roof, from which your father's body has been removed only for a time. Let me instruct one of my men to fetch your things.'

'Oh, very well.' Mark, Appleby reflected, had taken this stiff rebuke decently enough. 'But mayn't they want to turf me out?'

'You don't seem to realize your position, Mr Tytherton. I have been in touch with your father's solicitor. In fact he called here, at my request, half an hour ago. He saw your step-mother, and what he told her he decided he could then properly tell me too. Mrs Tytherton receives a reasonable jointure, and there are to be one or two other small charges upon the estate. Apart from this, it passes into your hands absolutely.'

'I see. And the chap has gone away?'

'The solicitor? Yes. But if you want –'

'Good. I've been telling Sir John I don't want my hand held. Not even by him, just at this stage. Any Let-me-be-your-Father stuff had better be out for the time being.' As he made this odd speech Mark looked at Pride squarely. 'Will you take me to your Inspector, please? I've one or two things to say.'

'Come with me now, Mr Tytherton.'

And the Chief Constable marched the young man within the portals he had just inherited.

'Not sitting in on this, John?' There was mild reproach in Pride's voice when he returned.

'Well, I wasn't wanted by that young man, was I? And I think that, as a matter of fact, a roving commission will suit me best this afternoon.'

'Fair enough. Henderson won't mind. Sign of confidence in him, really. I say, did I give away that there was more behind this lawyer's visit than I let on?'

'I wondered a little, I confess. These chaps don't commonly have much to say before the funeral and whatever baked meats follow upon it. He took the initiative?'

'The moment he heard about Tytherton's death this morning. Respectable old character called Pantin. Pantin and Pantin. Sounds a bit breathless, eh? Old-established local firm.' Colonel Pride was taking his customary pleasure in having made a joke. 'He called up the police, and made a point of contacting me personally. So I had him come over. He saw the widow, and so on, just as I said. But he also told me something pretty stiff. Maurice Tytherton rang him up at his house late yesterday evening, and asked him to come out to Elvedon this afternoon. Just live in a grand enough way, John, and you can treat a professional man as if he were the fellow who comes to tune the pianos or attend to the clocks.' Pride paused for a moment on this just sociological reflection. 'Tytherton wanted to draft a new will.'

'And what could be more classical than that?' Appleby, not given to gesticulation, had made a gesture of impatience. 'An almost infallible way to get yourself murdered, wouldn't you say? Almost as infallible as having an alienated heir skulking in the ha-ha, or disguised as a hermit in the Gothic cow-house.'

'Yes, of course.' Pride was conceivably a little at sea before this fantasy. 'But that's not all.'

'Tommy. I've heard those words already in the course of this affair. But I am patient. Expound.'

'There was something else Pantin felt he ought to tell me. It seems there's far less money behind all this than you'd think. If Mark Tytherton is to keep Elvedon he'll have to be a deuced good manager. Thin ice, Pantin says. Damned thin ice for years. Bad buys in that picture-fancying line. Extravagant wife. Voracious top tarts. Shocking state of affairs.'

'Did Pantin get the impression that Tytherton was acting impulsively and in a passion?'

'Yes, he did. He says he made a note to put the brake on. Term lawyers use, it seems, when coping with the sudden whims of clients. Pantin got the notion that some specific upsetting thing had happened, and that Tytherton had lost his wool.'

'Did he gather just what change or changes in his will Tytherton wanted to make?'

'Not a thing.'

'It might have been something big, or it might have been something little?'

'I suppose so.' Pride had led Appleby into the hall, which presented its customary appearance of mysterious depopulation. He lowered his voice to combat its resonance. 'Come to think of it, you know, he might have been proposing to disinherit his son.'

'Would that have been legally possible?'

'Not perhaps all the way. Must be this and that tied up one way and another in a concern like this, eh? But at least something pretty shattering might be in his power.'

'Yes – but my instinct is rather against it.' Appleby had paused, frowning, before the ancestral Tytherton commemorated by Sir Thomas Lawrence. 'For one thing, it's a tricky thing to do – leaving an only son the proverbial farthing. It may result in enormous sums vanishing in bitter law-suits, which is a thought the wealthy hate like poison.

And, for another, people just don't, so far as my experience goes. Don't you agree?'

'Perfectly true.'

'They may hound the offending child from the family hearth with dreadful imprecations. But they don't go on to rob him of his patrimony. What about Miss Kentwell?'

'Good God! What can she have to do with it?'

'She appears to be some kind of charity tout. Suppose she had cozened Tytherton into believing he could get a life peerage, or some such nonsensical thing, on the strength of promising something spectacular to the Depressed Widows of the Higher Clergy –'

'My dear John, be serious. Tytherton was a man of affairs. He would know what happens, and what doesn't.'

'Well, say at least that he had made some bequests of the kind. And that now, being hard up, he was thinking better of them. And suppose Miss Kentwell is in these matters a straight fanatic –'

'War games.' Pride had suddenly chuckled. 'We were being made to play them before I left the army. Entertaining, of course, and calculated to sharpen the wits. You imagine some totally crazy thing, and then work out its consequences. But let's keep Miss Kentwell till after dinner.'

'I have a notion she may show up then.' Appleby said this soberly, and now he turned round to pace the hall. 'Even if not quite in the role I've been sketching for her. Of course it's probably true that this proposed change in Tytherton's will concerned some minor family matter. Or better, perhaps, domestic matter. What about that awful Mrs Graves? He'd had her, so to speak –'

'You bet he had.'

'I wasn't intending the phrase in quite that sense. He was suddenly disenchanted with her, and was going to see that she didn't get that two, or three, or five thousand pounds.' Appleby came to a halt. 'And there are probably other possibilities in the same area.'

'Shocking business, this.' Colonel Pride recurred to a familiar note. 'A gutter paper's holiday, eh?'

'Oh, undoubtedly. But, talking of Mrs Graves, your Mr Pantin didn't happen to murmur anything about family jewels?'

'As a matter of fact he did.' Pride stared at Appleby in astonishment. 'It was when he was being discreetly communicative on the theme of hard times among the Tythertons. Mrs Tytherton – Alice Tytherton – is rather given to jewellery, as I think I mentioned before. Owns a heap of them in her own right. But apparently, some time back, Tytherton infuriated her by announcing he'd sold a sizable packet of his own family ones. Pretty significant, I'd say, having to do that. You'd have to be at a loss for no more than a few thousand pounds, I'd suppose, before you adopted such an expedient. Not our world, my dear John.'

'Definitely not. But perhaps he hadn't sold them at all. Perhaps he'd given them to the slinky-kinky Mrs G. Or to one of Mrs G's predecessors. Or even, as a softening up measure, to some nice little woman he had lined up for the succession.'

'You do have an ability to touch a hard-boiled note, John. Comes of having worked in London and among the nobs, I suppose.'

'I'm just suggesting there's plenty of scope. For salacious conjecture, if you care to put it that way. And the jewels needn't even have been honest Tytherton heirlooms. They may have been the rightful property of Mrs Tytherton the First.'

'My dear chap, isn't your fancy rather running riot?'

'Well no, as a matter of fact. I'm on rather solid ground with this one. But perhaps that's another story.'

'Another story?'

'Or say a related one. An *Arabian Nights* affair this, perhaps. Stories within stories. And we've got to sort them out.'

'By round about dinner-time, I think you said?' Colonel Pride allowed himself to import a faint sarcasm into this question.

'I'd hope so. But – do you know? – I think we mayn't even have touched the central one yet. There are people lurking in this house that I haven't yet so much as set eyes on. Two young men, for example – and a third whom I suppose to be a rather older one.'

'Meaning –?'

'The Tytherton nephew, Archie. The efficient chap who runs the place, and enjoys its vistas by moonlight.'

'Ronnie Ramsden.'

'And Mr Carter. The wholly nebulous Mr Carter, who seems to be hinted at as Alice Tytherton's consoler in hard times. Have you so much as a notion what he does with himself?'

'Yes, I have. It emerged not an hour ago. He's an eminent medical man.'

'You mean he's really not Mr Carter but Dr Carter?'

'Nothing of the kind. It's simply that he's a surgeon. Why one doesn't call a surgeon "Doctor" I don't know. But it's the English convention, is it not?'

'Yes, of course.' Appleby had spoken absently. Now, with alarming suddenness, he came to a dead halt. 'A surgeon, is he? That's as interesting as anything I've heard yet.'

13

Ramsden, the young man said to run Elvedon, was not hard to find. He had a kind of office in a semi-subterranean apartment which some predecessor of the Tythertons had caused to be tricked out as a small Gothic library; it was all fretwork and escutcheons, scraps of armour, pikes, halberds, and improbable looking wooden chairs and settles.

'I hope you don't find this room too silly,' Ramsden said easily. 'I'm rather at home in it. My very undistinguished school was in a house just like Elvedon – only four times the size – and our headmaster had a dungeon of a study much in this taste. When he had us in to correct us – which was his old-fashioned phrase – the effect of a mediaeval torture-chamber was pretty convincing. However, he was a civilized character, and always offered us a glass of sherry afterwards.'

'I think I'd have felt I deserved brandy.' Appleby had heard of this headmaster before, and realized that Ramsden, an employee at Elvedon, was urbanely planting his social credentials on the table. 'Were you, by any chance, at school with Mark Tytherton?'

'Yes, indeed. Mark and I were contemporaries.'

'Is that how you landed this job?'

'No, it had nothing to do with it. Pure coincidence. When I arrived at Elvedon six years ago, Mark had departed for the Argentine quite some time before. It was some weeks before I tumbled to the thing, or so much as remembered him.'

'Most interesting. Have you seen him lately?'

'No – in fact not since we left school. Of course I know he's back, and has been up to the house. But I haven't run into him. I think he's seeing one of the local policemen now. Probably Henderson, the chap I walked round with. And it's my turn next.'

'Ah, yes. There have to be formal statements from everyone.' Appleby offered this soothingly. 'And you don't object to a preliminary word with me?'

'Good Lord, no. Quite the contrary, Sir John. I feel this to be an occasion. Like meeting Bernard Shaw or T. S. Eliot.'

'Thank you.' Appleby received this mild impertinence unresentfully. The general posture of affairs at Elvedon no doubt put Ramsden, like everybody else, in one degree or other on the defensive. But he remained rather an attractive young man. His looks were in his favour, including a cool and candid gaze from clear grey eyes. His manners were all right and so was his manner – which was relaxed and easy, although neither of these things in excess. 'You and Miss Kentwell – about whom, by the way, I feel something a little odd – appear to have been last night's special case. You were in each other's company at the time of the killing, whereas everybody else appears to have been on his or her own.'

'Yes, until you get down to the servants. I suppose they oughtn't to be left out of the reckoning. For instance, the Catmulls. You know that Catmull, who is our butler, rejoices in a wife, who is our cook. They may have been in one another's company, for all I know. And so may some of the Italian girls.'

'Perfectly true – although I've no doubt that Inspector Henderson's people are checking up below-stairs too. But may I just stick to Miss Kentwell and yourself for a moment? I suppose you were *unintermittedly* within each other's observation throughout the relevant period?'

'Which you define as –?'

'From the moment of your together leaving Mr Tytherton's workroom when you had failed to find him to the moment of your together returning to it and discovering his body.'

'Then the answer is: Most certainly. We went up to the roof, you know, but there was no question of losing each other in the dark. Indeed it wasn't dark. There was a splendid moon.'

'So I gather. I suppose, by the way, that your view from up there took in pretty well the whole park. Did you happen to notice anything out of the way there?'

'You mean anybody moving around? No, I didn't. Was there anybody?'

'Well, yes.' Appleby had noted the adroit question. 'There was the vicar, looking for badgers. And there was Mark Tytherton.'

'Indeed.' Ramsden's tone was instantly one of disapproving reserve. 'I certainly saw nothing of Mark Tytherton. Nor of Voysey either.'

'There would only be an off-chance of it.' Appleby seemed to dismiss the point. 'But – by the way – if you *had* noticed somebody unidentifiable down there, would you have been at all perturbed?'

'Not in the least – unless the figure showed signs of prowling round the house. There's no right of way in the park, and we lock the gates once a year to safeguard the legal position. But Mr Tytherton never, so far as I know, took exception to local people taking one or another short cut through it at any time.'

'Ah, that brings me to something I find rather interesting. It may be called security. I'd have imagined that Tytherton *would* have been inclined to discourage any sort of trespass after his experience of robbery a couple of years back. That's an affair to which a good deal of fresh thought will have to be given. You must have considered, Mr Ramsden, the possibility that a second attempted burglary lies at the bottom of last night's tragedy?'

'I see the attractiveness of the idea – if that's not too awkward a way of putting it. But it's hard to see just how it could work out.' Ramsden frowned. 'The Goya, for example, up there in the workroom. It's not difficult to imagine Tytherton shot dead while defending it; shot dead as the result, say, of surprising a thief in the act.'

'Quite so. And the thief then got in a panic and fled.'

'But the hour is awkward, Sir John, wouldn't you say? Not yet midnight. It would have to be the small hours before anybody in his right mind would propose simply to take a great thing like that from the wall, tuck it under his arm, and march out of Elvedon with it.'

'Fair enough. But he might be proposing simply to open the window and lower the thing down to an accomplice.'

'An inside job – is that the phrase? But you know, Sir John, that a rough check has failed to show anything else missing. I went round with this Inspector or Superintendent who's going to see me again. A nice chap.'

'Henderson. Well, I'll tell you one thing he'll have before him by now – the police records of that first robbery. And he'll want your recollections of it.'

'He's welcome to them, Sir John. And I very much hope you're both on the right track.'

'Thank you.' For a moment Appleby had taken this as being merely a conventional expression. Now he looked sharply at Ramsden. 'Am I to attach some meaning to that?'

'I think you can guess what's in my mind.' Ramsden had

stood up, and was leaning over the back of a chair which would have served as a very adequate throne for King Lear in an aggressively antiquarian production of his tragedy. 'Robbery ending in murder is a pretty lurid affair. It's horrifying, or catastrophic, or sad, or whatever. But it's not dead squalid and scandalous.'

Ronnie Ramsden, Appleby reflected, appeared to own the same distastes as Colonel Pride. Robbery with violence was one thing; adultery and miscellaneous fornication with violence was quite another. But it would be as well to check that this really was what ran in the young man's head.

'Do I understand you to mean, Mr Ramsden, that other readings of Mr Tytherton's death are likely to require the sifting of a great deal that is unsavoury and immoral?'

'Well – that, more or less. I don't know about immoral. I don't think I'm particularly a puritan about a bit of bed-hopping, and all that. But it does get fearfully boring – a gang of people, some of them not even all that young, loosing their unbeautiful natures at each other and scrapping away over that sort of thing.'

'You'd rather they filched each other's Goyas, revolver in hand?'

'I'd call that an extravagant way to put it. But I suppose it's more or less what I mean.'

'It's an interesting ethical point of view.' Appleby spoke drily. 'But a picture-theft can be scandalous too, wouldn't you say? For instance, when it isn't one.'

'I beg your pardon?' The young man had sat down again – behind a desk of decidedly orderly character. He had suddenly taken on the air of one who had just so much time for Appleby, and no more. 'Will you explain yourself?'

'Certainly. I haven't yet got the facts, so this is only

conjecture. What I *have* got is the impression that the whole affair went in rather a minor key, was distinctly soft-pedalled – or any other metaphor you choose.'

'Just what affair, Sir John?'

'The supposed robbery two years back.'

'The *supposed* robbery?'

'That's where I just conjecture. By the way, I think I am correct in supposing that you manage the Elvedon estate, and a good many related matters?'

'I do.'

'Then it couldn't possibly be news to you that Maurice Tytherton's financial affairs have been more or less seriously embarrassed for some time?'

'It couldn't possibly be something I would discuss with you, Sir John.' Ramsden's reply had been swift and tart. 'You would have to apply to Mr Tytherton's solicitor.'

'The Chief Constable has already done so, and I think we have enough to go on. Are the pictures and so on here in Elvedon insured?'

'Yes, they are – although it costs the moon.'

'Those that disappeared a couple of years ago were insured?'

'They were, although not adequately.' Ramsden sat back squarely in his chair, his hands clasped on the desk in front of him. Although young, he looked formidable. 'Sir John, you are advancing a very grave allegation – and through the singularly odd medium of an informal conversation with myself. You are saying, in effect, that the late Mr Tytherton, some two years ago, stole certain of his own pictures, collected insurance money on them, and then presumably quietly sold them on some illicit market. Moreover you are suggesting that something of the same kind has in some mysterious fashion resulted in Mr Tytherton's death now. Am I right?'

'Yes, you are – provided you bear in mind that it is my common method in affairs of this kind to advance and review every conceivable hypothesis. I am perfectly willing to take up the sort of conjectures which you yourself appear more inclined to entertain. Some of them would be little more to Mr Tytherton's credit than is the theory I have just sketched. They will, of course, take longer to run over – and for an obvious reason.'

'Indeed?' Ramsden had perceptibly relaxed. 'May I ask what it is?'

'On the immediate horizon, I'm not aware of anybody who is at all intimately concerned with pictures except the man Raffaello. His presence at Elvedon has struck me a good deal, I'm bound to say. But he's a single spy, so to speak – whereas on the other side of the account there are battalions.'

'The other side of the account?'

'Or the column in which we reckon up the number of people showing signs of involvement in one or another sexual intrigue – and therefore very conceivably entangled in some drama of the sort which has had a fatal ending. This is really what you are saying yourself, I think.'

'I suppose it is.' Ramsden's grey eyes had clouded; he was looking at Appleby sombrely. 'But other possibilities remain. Sexual passion, after all, isn't the only sort of passion – I mean passion as distinct from calculation and cupidity and so on – that can lead to some fatal act of violence.'

'Certainly not sexual passion narrowly regarded.' Appleby paused; his own gaze upon Ramsden was speculative and intense. 'Sexual nausea, for example. Think of Hamlet.'

'I am not Prince Hamlet, nor was meant to be.' Suddenly Ramsden's expression changed, and he sprang to his feet. 'My God – you're thinking of Mark!'

'Who is said to have a thing about his mother.' Appleby spoke coldly. 'Is it *you* who are thinking of Mark?'

'In a way, yes. You yourself have gone out of your way to let me know that Mark was around Elvedon last night. What if he found the body – minutes before that woman and I did?'

'Just *found* it?'

'Yes – and in Tytherton's hand was the gun with which he'd killed himself. Why *shouldn't* he have killed himself? One way and another, he was in a considerable mess – as you and those policemen appear to have nosed out. But it's not a pretty thing for one's father to do. Better to die, say, defending the *lares et penates* – or the Goya. So Mark picked up the gun, and departed as he had come.'

'You don't seem to be too bad at conjectures yourself, Mr Ramsden. And if you ask me whether, at the moment, I possess a single fact that contraverts that little theory, I have to confess that I do not.'

14

All the same, I have a hunch – Appleby told himself as he prowled Elvedon. Maurice Tytherton assuredly did not blow his own brains out. If his story is to have a surprise ending it won't be that one. It may be true that the man was in a deepening mess, but it was a slowly deepening mess, not a sudden one. If he was hard up it was only in the sense in which the prosperous can be hard up. The need for embarrassing retrenchment may have been looming ahead, but he was never going to be in doubt about tomorrow's dinner. Or about tomorrow's Mrs Graves, for that matter. No, Tytherton had been murdered, all right. It just remains to spot by whom.

Appleby wandered up Elvedon's main staircase. It reminded him, incongruously, of Mr Voysey's delicately peeled apple, so elegant was its gentle spiral in finely chiselled Bath stone. Reaching the first floor, he walked down a cool corridor which seemed to stretch almost to a vanishing point before him. Embellished on one side by a long line of Flemish flower paintings of considerable merit, it displayed on the other, between high windows, a succession of console tables topped by fantasticated mirrors in the manner of John Linnell. They were like the ghosts of departed footmen, Appleby told himself, patiently doing nothing at all in the interest of the greater grandeur of some long since forgotten rout or soirée offered to the neighbouring notabilities by those first exalted Whigs who had built Elvedon.

It was doubtful whether he had any warrant thus to perambulate. Alice Tytherton would almost certainly consider it a vast impertinence. But Alice Tytherton was now, to put it crudely, a back number. If Elvedon ran to a dower house, that was what she was booked for. And it was for Mark Tytherton to say who went where. Indeed Mark, if the law didn't in one way or another interfere with his freedom of action, would have to decide what to do with the place. Perhaps he would settle down amid the paternal acres, shoot the pheasants, hob-nob with the neighbouring gentry and marry one of their daughters, become a magistrate or an M.P. Or perhaps things would turn out to be so bad on the financial front that he would be obliged to sell up and return to Argentina. In that event the Tytherton occupancy of Elvedon Court would have been an episode between its pristine glories and its final decline into a mental hospital or a disgraced mansion mysteriously necessary to the well-being of some hypertrophied public corporation.

With such reflections going through his head, Appleby shamelessly peered into one room or another. There was certainly no sign that Maurice Tytherton had been discreetly trundling his household chattels to the pawnbroker. Everything was as slap-up – Appleby wasn't sure that the vulgar expression didn't, somehow, fit – as in so imposing a country house it ought to be. And everything was on display. Only the door of Tytherton's workroom, which he came upon by chance and recognized, was locked. Henderson had now set up his headquarters elsewhere, no doubt.

There was still a notable absence of anybody around; Elvedon seemed to own a curious power of absorbing its occupants. He found a subsidiary staircase and went up to the next floor. The general effect here was identical, except that there was even less sense of any present human habitation at all. Or what there was, at least, was patchy: one principal corridor was uncarpeted and without any console tables presided over by gilded and rococo goddesses, huntsmen, stags, hounds, slaughtered wild-fowl, prodigal vegetation; some rooms were wholly unfurnished; it even all smelt a bit damp. Appleby recalled Alice Tytherton's disapproving sense that the Tythertons had never quite grown into the dimensions of the place. It wouldn't have been too easy to do, even in Victoria's middle time.

Appleby's meditations had advanced to this point when he turned a corner and bumped into Egon Raffaello.

It was an odd encounter, unexpected on both sides. Appleby even found it a little disconcerting, since he and this undesirable person were so demonstrably engaged in the same pursuit: that of quietly roaming through Elvedon for purposes of their own. Raffaello, indeed, since he was staying in the house, was perhaps behaving the less eccentrically of the two. He was also behaving after a fashion that Appleby had already heard of. Catmull had commented with disfavour on Raffaello's snooping round the place in a manner unbecoming in a gentleman. Catmull would presumably take a dark view of Appleby's present courses too.

'Good afternoon.' Appleby thought he had better move straight into the offensive. 'Are you running an eye over any unconsidered trifles – perhaps in the hope of snapping them up?'

'Snapping them up?' It didn't seem as if Raffaello made much of this innocent literary allusion.

'At the forthcoming sale, of course – if there is one. Something of the kind often follows a death in a household like this. It would be quite an event in your world, would it not?'

'No doubt.'

'And here you are, privileged to have a most valuable preview of what may go under the hammer. You must have given the whole house a pretty thorough once-over by the time you've come up here. Shall we go one higher? There's certainly another floor. Probably servants' rooms, for the most part, and largely empty. But one never knows what may be hidden where. At least that's what I feel about a house like Elvedon.'

'I don't care for your tone.'

'Never mind my tone, Raffaello. I've something to tell you that it may be useful you should know. In fact, several things. One is that the change of ownership of all this is an established fact. Tytherton's son inherits. There are legal formalities, of course. But in practice Mark Tytherton is the boss from now on. And he won't like you any more now than he did this morning. So you're on the way out. This may be your last snoop around. And I think I'm right in saying it hasn't got you anywhere.'

'And what about *your* snoop around? Has that got *you* anywhere?'

'Ah, that – my dear Raffaello – is confidential. I think Tytherton had rather baffled you? He'd been dangling possibilities that remained tantalizingly vague?'

'You know too much.' It was rather surprisingly that Raffaello said this unguarded thing. 'He was a tricky man to do business with. But there are plenty who are like that.'

'I don't doubt it for a moment. He was tricky when you did business with him before?'

'Before?'

'Come, come. You told me this has been your first stay at Elvedon, but you didn't say it represented your first acquaintance with Elvedon's owner. What about a couple of years ago?'

'A couple of years ago?'

'That's another of the things I have to tell you. There was a theft or robbery here, was there not? What I'd call rather a muted affair. But the police are interested in it again. They're *very* interested. The file is being reopened. And you know what happens when *that* takes place. Quite positively, my dear Raffaello, no stone is left unturned.'

'To hell with your stones. And I'm here on a proper social footing, Appleby. It's more than can be said of you. Not that that excludes professional services. I was to advise. I've been conducting expertises –'

'Absolute rubbish. You're a smart dealer, no doubt. But you have no scholarly authority whatever. I don't say you weren't competent to advise Tytherton what could be most profitably marketed where. But that's another matter.'

'Professional services.' Raffaello repeated this phrase with dignity. 'And I'll send in a bill.'

'I'm sure you will – and that it will be paid, worse luck. Unless we can land you in gaol first, my friend. One can send out bills from Wormwood Scrubbs. But they're not always attended to.'

'Quite a slanging match, this – isn't it?' Raffaello, although his confidence had been shaken, contrived a mocking note. '*You're* hanging around, Appleby. You're at a loose end. You're not getting anywhere.'

'In clearing up this murder? I wonder if you're right. But you'd like to see it cleared up, wouldn't you? It would take a weight off your mind?'

'It damned well would.'

'In which you are at one with all innocent persons – is that right? I'll do my best. But the solution of the affair – I warn you – may be attended by some inconveniences. Quite major inconveniences. Some of them may emerge when you and I have another talk.' Appleby looked at his watch. 'Perhaps some time after tea.'

'You're working to a time-table, are you?'

'Roughly speaking, yes. I'm getting rather more than middle-aged, you know. And I don't want this affair to keep me out of bed.'

'You seem very confident. I suppose it's part of your technique.'

'My technique is quite simple. It consists largely in persuading people that it's to their advantage to tell the truth. The graver the crime, the more obvious, surely, that is. I don't suppose people often get convicted of murders they didn't commit as a consequence of being insufficiently candid about precious little enterprises of their own. But it can land them in a very awkward situation. So oughtn't you perhaps to consider where you stand? You see, there's just nothing more coming your way in any case. Whether we wind the matter up briskly or not, this little house party will disperse as soon as the Chief Constable gives the word. And that will be immediately Inspector Henderson has finished taking his formal statements.'

'I know the law, Appleby. There's nothing to prevent any of us walking out of this damned house now.'

'Ah, but that's irrelevant, so far as you're concerned. You'd like to linger on – and you haven't a hope of it. You'll be shown the door, and whatever you've been hoping for here will be a complete write-off. I'm suggesting, therefore, that you cut your losses, come clean with a candid little account of yourself, and depart with an easy mind.'

'I don't know what you're talking about.'

'Yes, you do. I'm saying that Maurice Tytherton was up to something not too reputable, and was thinking, very appropriately, of enlisting the services of your shady self. But he dies leaving you in the dark – at least in some vital particular or other. You're still thinking that, if you can just find out, you may be able to extort some advantage from the situation. This, at least, is one way of looking at you.'

'What do you mean by that?'

'A charitable way of looking at you. The general situation I've sketched by no means precludes it's having been yourself who was constrained to put a bullet in the man. Just think! Here is Maurice Tytherton murdered literally under the eye of a Goya worth tens of thousands of pounds, and within a couple of years of some funny business with pictures transacting itself in this house. And here is Egon Raffaello, an art-dealer known to myself and others as enjoying uncommon luck in being still at large. It doesn't look pretty. Only let Inspector Henderson form a strong conviction about it, and you'll have a damned bad time. So my advice is simple. Go away and think it over. And don't spend too long on the job.'

15

More bullying, Appleby thought gloomily as he made his way downstairs. Boasting, too. All to be over by sundown. I wonder. Am I not still without so much as a glimpse of two possible star performers? But, ah! That looks like one of them.

The man with whom Pride was in conversation in the hall certainly had the appearance of a principal personage. A professional man, one would have said, in some distinctly prosperous mid-career. More carefully dressed, perhaps, than was altogether pleasing. Except that there was, so to speak, something to dress: a force and presence, a poise, which would have made themselves felt in dungarees. And his identity was confirmed by the Chief Constable at once.

'John, this is Mr Carter. Sir John Appleby.'

'How do you do?' Carter took a polite step forward, and shook hands with gravity.

'Mr Carter has been giving his account of things to Henderson, and he has an engagement in town this evening which he is anxious not to cancel. But he has heard that you are giving us a hand, and wonders whether he might have a short talk with you. He knows that Henderson welcomes anything of the kind.'

'But of course.' Appleby wondered what this somewhat unnecessary initiative on Carter's part portended. But it appeared to be a suitably gratified response that was expected, and this Appleby was very content to import into his tone.

'Nothing could be more valuable, Mr Carter, than your comment on this shocking business. Let us find a spot where we can sit down and talk it over. This hall strikes me as more imposing than comfortable, I'm bound to say.'

'The billiard-room,' Carter said unexpectedly. 'It doesn't sound promising. But nobody billiards here – except occasionally young Archie Tytherton by himself – and I've found it the most secluded place in the house. Come along, Sir John.'

A billiard-room is surely the most banal of apartments; this one was a little distinguished by displaying a large rural painting of the Dutch School. Three cows standing up, three cows lying down, a woman with a milking pail, and a river in a peaceful glow behind them.

'Cuyp?' Carter said, pausing before it. 'It's signed A.C., but if you ask me that means Abraham Calraet. But notice the triangular composition of the three creatures standing up. It's precisely the Three Graces, I'd say, or Giving and Receiving and Returning. You know the three ladies I mean: two frontal and one par derrière, wreathed in a dance? Haunted the artistic imagination for centuries, and got mixed up with the most abstruse Neo-Platonic speculation. Old cow-shed Cuyp wouldn't have made much of *that*. But here he is – or here's his imitator – all-unconsciously giving us that highly mystical conception in bovine terms. Quaint and interesting.'

'Very.' Appleby saw no occasion to elaborate this connoisseur's talk. 'Perhaps it was a common interest in artistic matters that made you and Maurice Tytherton congenial to each other?'

'Ah, yes – and other things.' Carter had slightly raised his eyebrows, as if indicating a sense that the pace was being a little forced. 'We had known one another for quite a long time.'

'But his friends in general –?'

'I beg your pardon?'

'Well, a few moments ago you happened to remark that you had found this the most secluded room in Elvedon. That suggests that you didn't find the society here wholly agreeable – or not, at least, more or less round the clock.'

'Perhaps so – yes. I haven't, as a matter of fact, stayed in this house all that often.'

'I see. You were not a sufficiently close friend of Maurice Tytherton's for his sudden death to have been a great personal shock to you?'

'True enough, Sir John. And I am, as it happens, rather used to sudden death. Or to sudden life, for that matter. Do you know, that can be almost as disconcerting?'

'Indeed?' It came to Appleby that the prosaically named Mr Charles Carter rather fancied himself as a conversationalist, and perhaps as a wit.

'By profession, as it happens, I am a surgeon. Sometimes sudden death is *there* – right under my hand. But sometimes the reverse obtains. There, on the table, is somebody who in all probability has three hours, an hour, half an hour to live. But one finds, against all expectation, that one can do this, or that – and to dramatic effect. With a few instruments gradually evolved from the butcher's shop I have created for this man further years of existence. Sudden life, in fact. And of course one wonders.'

'About the beneficence of what one has done?'

'Precisely. However, at least we don't yet traffic in an elixir or philosopher's stone. The conferment of immortality still eludes us. And while there is death there is hope.'

Appleby felt he had heard this little medical joke before,

but refrained from saying so. Instead, he moved abruptly to what he chiefly wanted to know.

'Mr Carter, was your original association with Maurice Tytherton a professional one?'

'He was never a patient of mine.' For a fraction of a second Carter hesitated. 'But his wife was.'

'Ah, yes. No doubt you mentioned this to Inspector Henderson.'

'I think not. It didn't crop up.'

'I see.' Appleby took a moment to study the Cuyp further. Carter had got away with something with Henderson; second thoughts had persuaded him he wouldn't continue to get away with it for long. 'Mrs Tytherton has mentioned to me that she underwent a serious surgical operation a little over two years ago, and that she recuperated from it in the South of France. That operation I take it you performed?'

'That is so.'

'And this would have been the occasion of your forming a first, or at least a closer, personal acquaintance with the Tythertons?'

'Quite so.'

'Mr Carter, are you fond of the South of France yourself? Do you perhaps go on holiday there?'

'Yes, I am – and I do. But I fail –'

'That may well have resulted in your visiting Mrs Tytherton during her convalescence?'

'I must protest against such questions. Their implication –'

'Oh, come. You are in danger of ceasing to be quite clear-headed – which I am sure is unusual with you. It's bound to come out, you know. That's why you have sought this interview with me. You feel, rightly or wrongly, that you and I talk more or less the same language, and that as a consequence aspects of the matter may be easier to sort out with me than with a rural police officer. I don't think there's

124

much in it. But, of course, I'm at your service, all the same.'

There was a silence. Carter had picked up a billiard-cue, and was idly taking aim at an ancient and somewhat discoloured white ball on the table. Perhaps his principal attraction – Appleby thought – was in those strong and beautiful hands. Appleby wondered what sort of hands Maurice Tytherton had possessed. Possibly Mrs Tytherton hadn't thought much of them.

'I'm naturally alarmed,' Carter said surprisingly. He executed a stroke with precision, and a series of swift clicks rewarded him. 'You can see why.'

'You possessed a very good motive for murdering Tytherton?'

'Oh, I hadn't quite thought of *that*!' Alarmed or not Carter looked up from the table with some appearance of amused astonishment. He was a handsome man. The wide expanse of fine cloth, reflecting the sunshine streaming in from a skylight, lent the flesh-tones of his face the greenish shades, one might say, of Correggio's nudes. 'We don't live in a novelette, with searing sensualities producing homicide at every turn. Tytherton was killed, I suppose, by somebody after his pictures. But any sort of irrelevant vulgar scandal is liable to be started up by such a thing – particularly as there has been this odd circumstance of his son's returning from South America and saying Lord knows what. It's oddly pat, I must say. Anybody would be prompted to rustle up a mystery out of it. And mysteries are news. And news battens on any scandal, however irrelevant, it can dig up.'

'There is undeniably much in what you say. To put it baldly, you are in a fix, and quite intelligent enough to be aware of the fact. However, I am in a position to offer you a word of encouragement. You are by no means singular. The number of people at present under this roof who are similarly circumstanced – in a fix, that is to say, on one account or another – may be fairly described as astonishing. I confess, however, that I find your own case a particularly interesting one. And I advise candour. I go round Elvedon, indeed, advising candour. But upon you, my dear sir, I positively urge it. Shall we face up quite squarely – you and I – to the special and peculiar occasion you may have felt for shooting down your host in cold blood? And I emphasize the temperature. Cold blood, not hot.'

'Just what do you mean by that, Sir John?'

'That is precisely the sort of question I am asked by one of the least attractive of your fellow-guests – the gentleman who calls himself Mr Raffaello. I regard the assumption of so divine a name as an outrage in itself. But that is by the way. I will tell you what I mean – and possibly launch a little straight talk as a result. You spoke just now, and in an ironic tone, of searing sensualities. Well, they do happen. And sometimes, when they have rather burnt themselves out, they leave an awkward legacy. Now, *don't* ask me just what I mean by that. We both know perfectly well. You lost your head over Alice Tytherton. You slept with her – regularly and often, I suspect – and now here you are, actually under her late husband's roof. Most unfortunately, she has been your patient. There you were, Carter, poised over her unconscious body and with those instruments of life and death in your hands. You did a good job by her – perhaps a quite notably good job. Sudden life, in fact. But then this thing happened. You seduced her. Or she seduced you. That's equally probable, I suppose. But the emotional niceties of the affair wouldn't much interest the General Medical Council.'

There was a short silence. Carter played another shot, and missed rather an easy cannon off the red. He made an impatient gesture, and thrust the cue back in its rack.

'Go on,' he said. 'You interest me. Are you supposing there was some sort of crisis yesterday?'

'It's a tenable view. I'm only dealing in tenable views.' Appleby had sat down in a deep arm-chair that exhaled a faint aroma of chalk and cigar-smoke. 'One is rather inclined to assume that Tytherton had been aware of your liaison with his wife for quite a long time; that he had tolerated it as belonging within the context of near-promiscuity which appears to have been the thing in his set. Certainly a lot of people were aware of it – including, I suspect, his own servants and tenants. Still, Tytherton *mayn't* have known. Or not to the extent of having proof. You may have been enormously careful. It was certainly very much in your interest to be so. Just get cited as co-respondent in a divorce suit in which the woman has been your patient, and your professional career is finished.'

'I grant you that one – as a general proposition, that is to say.' Carter, like Appleby, had sunk into a large chair. They might have been two idle denizens of this country house, gossiping their way through a boring afternoon. 'In more ways than one, my dear Appleby, my profession continues to drowse contentedly in the Victorian age.'

'No doubt. But now let me return to what I was speaking of: a possible action for divorce.'

'But you must know by now that Tytherton was what a judge might call a hardened adulterer. Even supposing your conjectures about his wife and myself to be true, he'd have found anything of the kind a tricky business to launch.'

'Perhaps so. A judge – since you are interested in judges – would certainly be unfavourably impressed by a plaintiff's admitting that he had brought a mistress – to wit, Mrs Graves – into his own matrimonial dwelling. Still, judges simply have to mop up these messes as best they can. Nowadays, they let what is called their discretion in such matters cover a great deal. So consider, Carter, where we are. Tytherton has either suddenly discovered the truth, or he has just got hold of what amounts to hard and fast evidence.' Appleby paused. 'So he sends for his solicitor. And gives himself the pleasure of telling you he has done so.'

'May I ask when you suppose this interesting event to have taken place?'

'Yesterday evening. And, this time, I am *not* supposing. I know Tytherton *did* send for his solicitor. The fellow's name is Pantin.'

'Well?' There had been a long silence in the billiard-room before it was thus broken by Carter's voice. 'Tytherton writes his letter. Or perhaps he simply telephones –'

'Yes. He telephones.'

'Yesterday evening, you say. So what follows?'

'I can leave that to your imagination. Or perhaps to your memory.'

'We'll say imagination, if you please. What follows is, I suppose, what you call the crisis.'

'Very definitely it is that. You get to know what he has done. Perhaps he simply tells you what he has done. Or there is another possibility – an ironical one.'

'I don't follow you.'

'Tytherton had occasion to contact his solicitor about something totally different. But doing so put it into his head to play an ill-natured joke on you. He told you he was about to institute divorce proceedings, although in fact nothing of the sort was in his mind. Probably he couldn't care less whether you were sleeping with his wife or not.'

'You are painting a picture of an extremely disagreeable group of people.'

'That's true, Mr Carter. I think I'd prefer to believe that he *had* just found out the truth, and *was* intending divorce.

Even if it wasn't the authentic occasion of his contacting Pantin there and then. However, the point is that you were convinced he had to be stopped. And there was only one sure way to do it.'

'To kill him?' As Carter asked this, he produced a cigarette and lit it with a steady hand.

'Yes. Dead men, they say, can tell no tales. It's equally true that they can start no law-suits. Nor can their heirs and executors – when all that's in question is a treacherous friend and a faithless wife.'

'You have a case.'

'Nothing of the kind. I repeat that I am only dealing in tenable views, and there are several more of them floating around. This particular one can possibly be rendered no longer tenable by something quite simple which you may now judge it sensible to say.'

'I didn't kill Maurice Tytherton. Is that any good?'

'It has its weight with me. But I think you will agree that it doesn't take us all that far. But there are a number of possibilities. According to Henderson's first information, you had gone off to bed, and were thus alone in your room, during the material time.'

'The material time?'

'Say, between eleven o'clock and eleven-thirty last night. But about this your recollection may have been – shall we say? – faulty. Perhaps you were in the company of somebody else – and thus have, in effect, some sort of alibi.'

'You do make me out to be a shady character!' Carter seemed genuinely amused. 'If I wasn't industriously murdering somebody, I was at least rampaging in my role as the celebrated adulterer, or perhaps merely seducing one of those attractive Italian maids.'

'May I suggest, Mr Carter, that this is no occasion for merriment?'

'How right you are. But about my movements last night I have nothing further that is helpful to say.'

'And nothing else whatever?'

'At least at this stage, no.' Charles Carter rose composedly to his feet. 'Except that, in the light of what you have been kind enough to suggest to me, Sir John, I think I shall cancel my evening engagement in town. It would be something of a rush now, in any case. Moreover, I am not sure that I might not feel a shade out of things.' And Carter glanced at his watch. 'Do you know,' he said, 'I believe there is now some prospect of tea?'

16

This proved to be not too sanguine an expectation. In a library which opened through high french windows upon the main terrace before the house tea was being dispensed to the company at large by a personage of no less consequence than Catmull himself. Perhaps he was making amends, Appleby thought, for having delegated to inferior hands the serving of that buffet lunch.

But the ritual of tea-drinking at four-fifteen in the afternoon (and this, however superior is the Lapsang Souchong, however thin the cucumber sandwiches, however delicate the breeze that ventures to stray indoors through filmy curtains from the golden glow without) is unlikely to be a wholly comfortable occasion when chiefly participated in by suspected murderers and variously graded officers of the police. Such conversation as was taking place fell noticeably short of that sparkle and elegance which might have been expected in a company of so notably polished – or at least prosperous – an order as now haunted Elvedon Court.

The efficient Ronnie Ramsden, it was true, found something to say as, seconding Catmull's more professional labours, he moved around in the interest of polite attentions to the ladies. The ladies, however, were unresponsive. Alice Tytherton, whose bearing before lunch might have been called aggressive, was now distinctly subdued. Carter had crossed the drawing-room and had a murmured word with her when he entered. Was she too now meditating the possible implications for herself of the suggestion that her husband had been considering the possibilities of divorce? Or even – to go back to what Appleby really knew – the advisability of changing his will? Under the existing will, as Appleby had heard, there was appropriate provision for her by way of jointure. Presumably Maurice Tytherton, had he wished, could have altered this in some way. The law would not have permitted him to leave his widow without a penny – or so Appleby as a layman supposed – but perhaps it had been in his power drastically to curtail whatever settlement he had made. In other words, once that particular alarm was started, once the abrupt summoning of Mr Pantin (of Pantin and Pantin) was known, Alice Tytherton was among those who might be favourably disposed to securing Maurice Tytherton's abrupt decease. Conceivably the fact of the police having tumbled to this simple point had come home to her.

Mrs Graves, too, was subdued – although not indeed in the aspect of *tenue*. The advancing cohorts of photographers conjured up for her by Appleby in the course of their curious encounter at the Hanged Man had evidently been in her mind when making a subsequent *toilette*. She would now cut a striking figure even in the most sensational public print. And she had, it was to be presumed, little to lose by appearing there. Perhaps she even had something to gain. Figure as a high-class courtesan in a sufficiently newsworthy situation and the most gratifying offers are likely to come pouring in. So why should she be glum – even (as Appleby sensed her to be) uncommonly scared?

Perhaps Mrs Graves had shot her lover. Perhaps she had walked into that workroom of Tytherton's, surprised him sitting at his writing-table, and put a bullet in his brain. But why – except that it was one of the far too numerous guesses it was possible to make in front of this unpleasing affair? Doggedly disposed to consider the problem, Appleby retreated, tea-cup in hand, into an embrasure between cliffs of books. There was the business of Mark Tytherton's mother's jewels. Suppose that they existed, and were not more or less a figment of that young man's heated imagination. Suppose that Maurice Tytherton had in some way contrived to hold on to them in an improper fashion after the dissolution of his first marriage. Indeed, something more than supposition was available here. Appleby had not himself encountered Pantin, but had no reason to suppose that he would be given to unfounded gossip about a client. It could at least be taken as assured that Tytherton had angered his second wife by telling her he had sold certain jewels she considered herself entitled to the enjoyment of. It was after *this* that conjecture really came in. *If* Tytherton had in fact given or lent these contentious objects to his latest mistress, and *if* there had been a further row about them, might this not conceivably have led Mrs Graves to some lethal extremity? It seemed not probable – but a possibility it certainly was. And when one brought into the picture the curious fact that his mother's jewels were an acknowledged obsession of the newly-arrived Mark Tytherton it did look as if they could not be far from the centre of the mystery.

Appleby abandoned this speculation for the moment. The relevant facts would come clearer if Mark Tytherton turned out to have been communicative with Henderson. And now his eye fell on the third of the ladies. Miss Kentwell was talking to Carter with an air of composed affability about which there was nothing obtrusive, but which yet somehow arrested Appleby's attention. She was like a cat, he told himself, that has decided to call it a day with a mouse. The image was an extremely odd one, and quite unsupported by any simple visual suggestion. Miss Kentwell was less like a cat than an over-fed canary, and Carter wasn't in the least like a mouse. But then every time Appleby thought about Miss Kentwell he was irked by a sense of something unaccountable about her. It was partly that he didn't quite believe in her charitable zeal, which seemed just a little too good to be true. And it was partly – as he had reflected before – that she was most unlikely to have gained the *entrée* to Maurice Tytherton's Elvedon on quite that ticket. She had insinuated that Tytherton had owned some notion that philanthropic gestures might get him into an Honours List, but the suggestion hadn't been a convincing one.

So mightn't all this have been a cover for something else? Once more Appleby glanced at the lady, and at Carter with whom he was sensing her to be in some equivocal relationship. A *post-bellum* relationship, he suddenly told himself. That was it. Mr Charles Carter, the eminent surgeon, was no longer Miss Kentwell's quarry.

Appleby was so pleased with this discovery that he looked round for somebody to whom he could communicate it. This, in the nature of the situation, could only be Colonel Pride or Inspector Henderson, and Pride had for the moment vanished. But Henderson was approaching him now, and with some air of requiring moral support. Henderson didn't feel this tea-party to be altogether regular. But in the company of Sir John Appleby, after all, he couldn't be going too far wrong.

'Henderson, come into this little retreat, and let us confer. We ought to have a certain amount of information for each other by now.'

'We'd have wasted an afternoon if we hadn't.'

'Good – but first tell me this.' Appleby put down his cup. 'That Miss Kentwell, there at the other end of the room. Have you discovered her profession?'

'Charity organizer.'

'Ah, yes – but anything else?'

'The only other thing I know about her – apart from her own account of her movements last night, and so on – is that the servants here don't like her a bit.'

'Catmull?'

'Both Catmull and his wife.'

'I see. I haven't yet met Mrs Catmull. I think I must seek her out.'

'That won't be difficult, sir. She's in the butler's pantry more often than not.'

'Her husband's pantry? But isn't she the cook?'

'I believe so. Perhaps she's scared. But about Miss Kentwell – some of the servant-maids don't care for her either. Foreigners, of course, they are; and perhaps one needn't much attend to them. But they say she spies on them.'

'On the maids themselves – those Italian girls?'

'Yes, sir – and in a general way as well. The young women sleep at the top of the house, and three nights ago one of them came down to the kitchens in the small hours. Catmull hadn't allowed her something she rather fancied at supper in the servants' hall, and she was determined to get the better of him and nobble some. A kind of jam-tart, I gather it was.'

'Good for her. Well?'

'She saw Miss Kentwell creeping round the house. She –'

'Bedroom doors – that sort of thing?'

'Yes, sir.' Henderson stared. 'Or so this young person says. She may have a nasty mind.'

'Nothing of the kind.'

'I'm sorry, sir.' Henderson was like a rock. 'Whatever the lady may have been up to, I have a strong impression that this girl was drawing on her imagination, at least to some extent.'

'It's immaterial, Henderson. There can't be any doubt about what the woman has been up to. Her role as a charity organizer or whatever is entirely spurious. And her real role, incidentally, makes it pretty certain that she didn't – that she and Ramsden between them didn't – kill Tytherton. Tytherton was her employer. He introduced her to Elvedon, in an entirely bogus character, to spy on his wife. He was meditating a divorce, and Miss Kentwell is nothing other than a private inquiry agent. And from some damned expensive firm, I don't doubt.'

'I see, sir.' Henderson said this a shade woodenly. 'And it would be Carter who is in question?'

'Yes, Carter – the fellow she's innocently chatting up now. Her assignment is over, after all.' Appleby paused. 'Not that Alice Tytherton mayn't have been admitting other lovers. So Miss Kentwell may have enjoyed what might be called a roving commission.'

'It seems to me, sir, that the Chief Constable is pretty well right about this lot.' Henderson grimly surveyed the tea-party at large. 'Live like cats, it seems. But it may all be a bit aside from our concern.' Henderson hesitated. 'You see, Sir John, it's rather my instinct to cling to the pictures as the mainspring of the affair. If Miss Kentwell had been prowling Elvedon suspiciously, so has Raffaello –'

'That's absolutely true.' Appleby's admission was immediate. 'And it's certainly not something to lose sight of.'

'Well, we do know where *his* interests lie. He may have made brief passes at Mrs Graves –'

'Not significant, I agree. She's a loose woman, and asks for it.'

'Just so, sir. And if Raffaello is near the centre of the thing, then the pictures are.' Henderson hesitated. 'And you see, sir, in my own mind, I keep on coming back to the one in the dead man's room.'

'Ah, the Goya. A splendid portrait.'

'I'd be right, I take it, to suppose it very valuable?'

'Certainly. At a guess, I'd say it's the most valuable thing in the house.'

'Then Tytherton's being killed right in front of it looks to me like being significant.'

'But it's there on the wall still, quite undisturbed.'

'Yes, Sir John – it's safe and sound, all right. But I have this thought about something unexpected having perhaps disturbed somebody's programme. I know it sounds a trifle vague, that.'

'Not at all. And I'd be inclined to call something of the sort inherently probable. We're dealing with more than one story, as I think I've said. So why shouldn't one of them, so to speak, blunder in on another?'

'Well, sir, grant me that, and I'll ask you about something else. We got it clear, you remember, that if Ramsden and Miss Kentwell hadn't happened to go back to the work-room, nothing out of the way might have been discovered until this morning. Even after Tytherton was shot – always provided the shot hadn't been heard – there would have been a useful space of time in which to make a clean getaway with the picture. Not only off the premises, but a good deal further.'

'Anything up to twelve hours.' Appleby shook his head. 'Useful – but not all that useful.'

'May I ask, sir, just what sort of conditions you'd relish, if you had a mind to steal a picture like this Goya yourself?'

'I can tell you at once.' Appleby was amused by so hypothetical a question. 'I'd like something between a week and a fortnight to elapse before the theft came to light at all. It would give me a chance of selling the thing – in a quiet way, of course – more or less on an open and legitimate market.'

'To an unwary but *bona fide* purchaser?'

'Just so. Once the theft was news, it wouldn't be so easy – not by a very long way. But all this is a trifle irrelevant, isn't it? In the circumstances we confront in relation to Tytherton's Goya, it's hard to work out how anybody could be planning anything of the kind. For how could it be done?'

There was a pause. Appleby had been looking a shade absently at Henderson as he spoke. Equally absently, his eye now roved over the assembled company, just comfortably out of earshot.

'They're a mixed lot, aren't they?' Henderson said.

'I beg your pardon?' Appleby had turned back with a start. 'Sorry! I was remembering something – and from rather a long time ago. Yes, thoroughly mixed. One of them, by the way, definitely knows about pictures and so on. The distinguished sawbones, Carter. The others, I'd suppose, don't much go in for that kind of thing.'

'The one I'm worried about, sir, is young Mr Tytherton. The heir, that is : Mr Mark Tytherton. His story – and I've had a story from him – doesn't seem to hitch on to the picture-business. It takes us back to all this damned whoring.'

Henderson had been suddenly vehement – but apparently more out of intellectual irritation than moral repugnance.

'You take Mark Tytherton to be given to that sort of thing?' Appleby asked.

'Not at all. Of course we don't know anything about his way of life. But at least nothing he's said suggests any concern to get into bed with anybody. It seems rather that the whole spectacle – even from thousands of miles away – had been getting him down. And particularly what he calls the ultimate insult in the matter of his mother's jewels. He *is* a bit cracked about that.'

'Yes. But what's now his full story?'

'It's extremely simple. He walked over to Elvedon at about ten o'clock last night, saw a light in his father's work-room, and came straight into the house. It hadn't yet been locked up. He went upstairs and presented himself. He says he thinks his father wanted to receive him decently, but was very upset.'

'About Mark's unexpected arrival?'

'Not that at all. He's quite positive. It was as if his father had just received, and hadn't recovered from, some considerable shock. His father was in what he called a bate, meaning a rage. So –'

'Did they have a drink together, all the same?'

'Yes, they did. But then the meeting went badly wrong. Mark says it was as if his father's bate was catching. He – Mark, that is – started in on this jewels business, said he wouldn't stand for their being handed round a brothel –'

'Strong words, Henderson.'

'Yes, sir. He demanded that they be given up to him, and his father said it couldn't, or wouldn't, be done. It was all quite horrible, Mark says, and over in ten minutes. He stormed out of the house, still without seeing anyone, wandered about the park for a long time, and then went back to his pub. That's his whole story.'

'Well, well. It's at least clear, is it not, to what it directs us?'

'Sir?'

'To the only chief performer in this sordid tragi-comedy that I haven't been able to introduce myself to. Is that him over there – the pasty-faced youth?'

'That is the dead man's nephew, sir. Mr Archie Tytherton.'

'He looks unhealthy.'

'I doubt whether it's to be called a natural pallor. He was

extremely nervous when I first saw him and he told me that story about a nightmare.'

'Ah, yes – the giant billiard-balls.'

'And it seems to me that his terror has been growing ever since.'

'He's another who's in a fix, of course.' From across the big library, Appleby regarded Archie Tytherton attentively. He was standing by himself, automatically gulping tea. 'He, too, had his row with Maurice Tytherton yesterday evening. This seems an uncommonly quarrelsome house, wouldn't you say, Henderson?' Appleby didn't pause for a reply. 'Only, this young man's row was before Tytherton rang up his solicitor, whereas Mark's was after it. By the way, wasn't Archie's row with his uncle witnessed by somebody?'

'That was Catmull. Catmull claims – but I can't say that I regard him as very reliable – that he overheard Maurice Tytherton, in a great fury, say something to his nephew about having caught him with his pants down.'

'An ambiguous expression, it seems to me.'

'Yes, sir. It is a common figure of speech for mere un-preparedness, I believe. But in this instance it might have had a rather –'

'Quite so. I really must attempt conversation with Archie Tytherton.'

17

Appleby made the attempt forthwith. But he had no sooner moved out of his corner of the library than he became aware that the late Maurice Tytherton's nephew must have been keeping an apprehensive eye on him. The young man was now making for the door. Appleby felt a certain sympathy for him. Archie had twice been carpeted by Inspector Henderson, and it wasn't perhaps unreasonable in him to feel that this was enough. Moreover that he was in a fine state of panic was attested by the precipitate clumsiness of his present retreat. He had put down his cup and saucer with an unseemly clatter, and had then stood so little upon the order of his going that he had bumped into Mrs Graves quite violently from behind. Mrs Graves had turned and glared at him; they had glared at each other, indeed, with a curious and disagreeable intensity of regard; and then the unappealing Archie, with one further panic-stricken glance at Appleby, had bolted from the room.

Appleby followed, more decorously but with almost the same speed. At least he was out of the library in time to see that Archie, swayed perhaps by the cunning of a hunted creature, had turned not towards the other principal apartments of the mansion but down a short passage leading to its domestic offices. What was now going forward was, frankly if absurdly, a pursuit. When Archie vanished through a green-baize door of the free-swinging sort which prescriptively segregates from their betters the menial

hordes of a house like Elvedon Appleby was so close behind him that the rebound of the contraption almost caught
him on the nose. This was not a major check; nevertheless
when he had coped with it and plunged into a further passage it was to find that Archie had vanished. He could
certainly not have reached its other end, so he must have
dashed through one near-by door or another. Appleby
chose the one closest to him, threw it open without ceremony, and entered the room thus revealed.

What he first became aware of was a culinary object
which he had no difficulty in identifying as a rolling-pin. He
next observed that a certain amount of flour and even
pastry still adhered to its surface. Finally, he realized that
this normally harmless implement was being employed as a
weapon, and seemed about to come down on his head.

Keep up your bright swords, for the dew will rust them.
Appleby must, he supposed, have contrived some such
injunction as this, although phrased more prosaically. For
the lady with the rolling-pin (who could only be Mrs
Catmull, thus emblematically armed, like a saint carrying
the appropriate instrument of her martyrdom) set it down,
albeit reluctantly, on a table chiefly furnished with cloths,
brushes, and silver-polishes. Appleby was constrained to
realize that he had unwittingly blundered into what was a
sanctum indeed. Here was the pantry of Mr Catmull himself.

'What you doing here?' Mrs Catmull demanded. Her
tone suggested much more of truculence than of the reasonable deference prescriptively required of her when suddenly
confronted by somebody of superior social station. 'You've
no business here, you haven't – nor has anyone except this
new Mr Tytherton himself. And the good manners to keep
away, he's had, he has.'

'I'm sure that's most commendable.' Appleby recalled Catmull's derogatory attitude towards his wife's degree of educational accomplishment. 'And I'm very sorry to intrude upon you in this way. I thought I was going to find Mr Archie Tytherton.'

'If you want *him*, sir, you can have him, so far as I'm concerned. But he wouldn't be welcome in this pantry of my husband's, he wouldn't. Nothing but a paratroop, that young Mr Archie is, nor ever was anything else.'

'A hanger-on, Mrs Catmull?' It was only for a moment that Appleby had been baffled by the apparent ascription of the career of arms to Archie. 'Living on his uncle, would you say?'

'His late uncle. This new Mr Tytherton, he'll give him the right-about, I shouldn't be surprised.'

'I see. Well, my conversation with Mr Catmull earlier today suggested, I'm afraid, that he was a little apprehensive of receiving the right-about himself. He resents the possibility – very naturally, I should say, considering how snugly he's accommodated here.'

As he thus enlarged the scope of his conversation with the lady, Appleby glanced round the pantry. In this *adytum*, he recalled, Catmull had asserted that all his worldly possessions had their sanctuary. It was a fairly big room, and with a certain amount of furniture, largely in abraded leather, of the sort that upper servants do over a period of years collect from indulgent employers. But perhaps its most prominent object was one which would have startled and not much pleased the Reverend Mr Voysey: a stuffed badger to which some rustic taxidermist had ingeniously imparted a quite needless air of extreme ferocity. For the rest, it might have been conjectured that Catmull shared with his late master a decided taste for the graphic arts. In a position of honour over the large safe in which

143

the butler presumably kept the Tytherton silver hung an enormously blown up photograph, in dingy sepias, of some departed Catmull ancestor. Standing on one foot only, with just the toe of the other elegantly touching the ground, and supporting an elbow on a kind of up-turned drainpipe topped by a fern, he was in fact the Catmull equivalent – Appleby reflected – of that Tytherton whom Sir Thomas Lawrence had depicted gesturing at a ledger. But apart from this exhibition of family piety, Catmull's taste appeared to incline towards pugilism and the turf, since the dozen or so other pictures, displayed in heavy and hideous frames of some ebony-like substance, were prints of improbably elongated race-horses and all too persuasively gory prize-fights being fought out for the delectation of assembled groups of gentlemen upon grassy swards and amid surroundings of rural calm. Appleby turned away from these evidences of connoisseurship in the interest of furthering his acquaintance with their proprietor's spouse. Archie Tytherton had eluded him for the moment, but it ought not to be difficult to run him to earth later.

'Your husband,' he said with mild geniality, 'tells me that you've read about me in a book.'

'Ah, then you're him I thought you might be – Sir John Appleby.' If Mrs Catmull was impressed to a gratifying degree it was also true that a certain air of suspicion which emanated from her seemed not wholly abated. 'It's not proper,' she went on, 'what's been happening at Elvedon. Not proper at all. Shooting poor Mr Tytherton like that – a perfect gentleman in every way, sir –'

'You had a high regard for your employer?'

'Well, now – not that he wasn't a shocking old goat, begging your pardon. But very correct as a gentleman in every way, and this shooting of him like a dog is a very bad thing. But that's not all.'

'Ah – these, Mrs Catmull, are familiar words. But to just what do you refer?'

'The foreigners, sir. Not respectable company any way on. Peering and spying, like I've no doubt you've heard. The one called Raffaello. Caught him in this very pantry, we did – which is why I now give a hand to Catmull keeping an eye on it.'

'And with a rolling-pin. Well, well. But what do you suppose Mr Raffaello to have been after here?'

'The spoons, I'd say, or anything he could lay his hands on. Taken into custody, he should be, and remanded and all that, and put away proper.'

'I'm not altogether unsympathetically disposed to that point of view. But did you say "foreigners"? You surely don't regard Mr Mark Tytherton as a foreigner simply because he has lived for a long period overseas?'

'Certainly not. An empire-builder in the Queen's dominions, Mr Mark has been – and had a very civil word with me not an hour ago.'

'I'm delighted to hear it.' Appleby refrained from a discussion of the political status of Argentina. 'So who –'

'The other prowler and peeper. Her as calls herself Miss Kentwell.'

'I've heard something about her prowling and peeping. But *isn't* she Miss Kentwell? I confess she doesn't suggest herself as a foreigner to me, Mrs Catmull.'

'Then with respect, sir, you don't know what you didn't ought not to be aware of.' Mrs Catmull paused on this syntactically complicated reproof. 'A Russian Bolshevik, she is, and nothing else. Kentwell! If you ask me, Kentwellski's her middle name.'

'You astonish me, Mrs Catmull.' Appleby was able to reflect that this was literally true. He wondered whether Mrs Catmull's cooking was as bizarre as what appeared to go on inside her head. 'Suspicion has been more or less my trade. But here is something which, I must confess, has totally eluded me.'

'I know what I know.' With this gnomic utterance, Mrs Catmull's own suspicions seemed to deepen – as they well might while Appleby allowed himself this ironical vein. 'And so does others in this house. Them girls.'

'Ah, I'd forgotten. Your housemaids, and so on, make up quite a little colony of foreigners.'

'And very well-conducted young persons they are. No trouble with the outside men – or not that they're so careless as to let you hear of.' Mrs Catmull paused on this generous encomium. 'On account of the Pope of Rome, that is. Keeps them properly in order, he does. What they do, they have to confess. And when he doesn't like it, he slaps them down hard.'

'It sounds an admirable system. But just what are you telling me, Mrs Catmull, about Miss Kentwell and these Italian girls?'

'There's one of them does her room. And tidies her drawers.'

'Garments, Mrs Catmull?'

'Chests of drawers, and the like, sir.' Mrs Catmull showed some sign of being offended by this wanton indelicacy. 'Part of their proper duties, that is. And taught them myself, sir – which is no part of a cook's junction, as you'll admit. But junctions get mixed up, when you're in service as a married couple.'

'It seems undesirable in junctions. But just what did this rummaging in drawers produce?'

'Excommunications from the Kremlin.' Mrs Catmull paused, as she very justly might upon such an astounding announcement. 'The same being clear,' she added a shade bathetically, 'through having Russian stamps.'

'Miss Kentwell gets letters from Russia. Is that what you are telling me?'

'Not sent to her at Elvedon, they weren't. Brought them with her, she must have done. And hidden away in a wallet.'

'It was obliging of the young Italian lady to tidy her wallet. Have you seen any of these letters yourself?'

'I have not – nor would be the wiser either, seeing they must be in a heathen tongue. But there was no doubt about the stamps, this girl says. Hammers and sickles all over them.'

'If Miss Kentwell was indeed an emissary of the Kremlin, Mrs Catmull, it was rather careless of her to be carrying such letters around with her. And even odder that she should have received them through the post at all. Incidentally, how would you account for the late Mr Tytherton's having admitted such a person into his house?'

'She infiltrated, that's what she did.' Mrs Catmull paused again. 'Catmull's word,' she said. 'He's an educated man, he is. Means no more than making coffee to me.'

'Mr Tytherton would have been unaware of her true identity and purpose?'

'Just that. Thought her one sort of spy, he'd have done. And all the time she was another.'

'I see.' Despite the lunatic cast of Mrs Catmull's mind, Appleby was rather impressed by this. 'So what do you think should be done?'

'An importation order – that's what she needs.' Mrs Catmull was incisive. 'An importation order, and put on the first plane available. And that Raffaello gaoled, like I said. It would be the beginning of a clearance, wouldn't it?'

'A clearance which you would then like to see continue?'

'Well that's Catmull's idea. After all this, he says, they ought to leave the place to ourselves. It's quite often done, he says.'

'I was remarking something of the sort to him earlier today.'

'That's right. While the lawyers and probate people do their work, and that. Not that I take account of such things.'

'Ah, yes. Everything will have to be valued, no doubt. And in a place like Elvedon, that is liable to take quite a lot of time.'

'Well, they're not coming in here, they aren't.'

'I am sure, Mrs Catmull, they will not be so discourteous. And I must apologize for my own intrusion. You will no doubt be having to think of dinner.'

'A saddle of mutton, sir, and the peas and beans our own, I'm thankful to say – and the same going for the basil for the tomato salad. It all takes some preparing, it does, for a company like the present – and me with no more than a couple of girls from the village to help me, so far as all the kitchen work goes. May I make bold to ask if you will be dining yourself? In which event I'd manage a soufflé, sir, if your taste was such.'

'That's most obliging of you.' Appleby was surprised and gratified by this signal mark of favour. 'But I shall be going home to dinner, although I may return to Elvedon later. And now I must continue my search for Mr Archie Tytherton.'

'Ah, him! I'd look under the beds, if I was you. Treacherous, is that young man. Treacherous as a sparrow.'

'I believe I understand you, Mrs Catmull. Has he been a nuisance to the maids?'

'A nuisance to the pigs and the chickens, he'd be, if you gave him half a chance at them. Even made passes at me, he has.' It was with no particular appearance of humility that the robustly spoken Mrs Catmull appeared thus to rate herself below the beasts of the field.

'I am very sorry to hear it, Mrs Catmull. My advice is to take that rolling-pin to him, should he think to annoy you again. However, I judge it probable that, for some time, other matters will be occupying his mind.'

18

The company had dispersed from the library, with the sole exception of Miss Kentwell. The emissary from the Kremlin sat in a window embrasure, engaged in a task of embroidery. It occurred to Appleby that it might not be entirely without profit to have a word with her before resuming his quest of the elusive Archie.

'Good afternoon,' he said. 'What a charming design, and how delicate the execution! I see that you are a person of aesthetic sensibility. Elvedon and its treasures must hold a great deal of interest for you.'

For the first time in their admittedly scant acquaintance, Miss Kentwell looked at Appleby with a hint of suspicion and even of alarm. He had already, he remembered, congratulated her on being a woman of iron nerve, and it was not unreasonable that this further absurdity should puzzle her.

'Thank you,' Miss Kentwell said. 'But I have few pretensions, Sir John, of the sort you suggest. My embroiderywork is undertaken for charity. The Society for the Suppression of Savage Customs. It has lately been making great headway, I am glad to say.'

'Has it, indeed? You surprise me. And you do seem to have a variety of calls of this sort upon your time. You must be anxious by now to conclude your visit to Elvedon, with all its distressing associations, and return to your customary fields of philanthropic endeavour.'

'That, of course, is true.' Miss Kentwell inclined her head sedately. 'But I plan, in fact, to stay on for a few days. Mrs Tytherton, indeed, does now have her delightful step-son to support her. But feminine counsel has its special place in times of sorrow.'

'There is Mrs Graves, however. Would you say she might serve?'

'I fear, Sir John, that Mrs Graves is not a person whom we ought to discuss.'

Appleby accepted this rebuke with a good grace. He was wondering whether he had, somehow, got Miss Kentwell wrong. If she had really come to Elvedon for the reason he supposed – as a private inquiry agent hired by Maurice Tytherton to spy upon his wife – it was odd that she was now parading what was plainly a wholly fictitious reason for lingering any longer in the house. The Catmulls wanted to linger – whether as a matter of professional security or in order to have the opportunity for a little quiet thieving. The tenor of Catmull's artless questions, indeed, rather powerfully suggested the latter motive. Raffaello wanted to linger – and almost certainly to pursue some better informed and more considerable act of depredation. But why Miss Kentwell? Appleby noted the question as worth meditating, and turned to something else.

'Miss Kentwell, I am sure you have been most helpful to Inspector Henderson in his inquiries. But I wonder whether you would answer one or two questions which have occurred to me as well? They may really be called time-table inquiries, and they stem from my feeling that quite a number of things – really, of disconnected incidents – may have fitted themselves into a very short interval last night. And into one definite place: Maurice Tytherton's work-room.'

'That is precisely my own view.' Miss Kentwell checked

herself – conceivably, Appleby thought, because she detected this speech of hers as having been a little out of character. 'But my mind is not at all clear about it all. It is so shockingly remote, Sir John, from anything within my experience hitherto.'

'That I can well imagine. But my principal question is simply this : on the first occasion that you went into Tytherton's workroom, and found it untenanted, how long did you and Mr Ramsden remain there?'

'I'm afraid I find that hard to say.'

'Perhaps you can arrive at an approximate answer by recalling the sequence of your actions, or for how long you were engaged in any one of them. For example, did you spend a little time looking at the Goya?'

'The what, Sir John?'

'The picture over the mantelpiece : a portrait of a man, by the Spanish painter, Francisco Goya.'

'Oh, yes – I think I have heard of him. And I suppose – now you mention it – that Mr Ramsden may have meant to draw my attention to the picture. I certainly didn't spend any appreciable time studying it. But now I *can* remember something I did – or thought of doing. Lighting a cigarette. There was a glass box with cigarettes on the mantelpiece –'

'I remember that.'

'And I thought I'd take one. That was why I put down my bag, when I come to think of it. You will remember about my bag. I put it down just where, on my return to the room, the tray with the brandy was standing.'

'Ah, yes. And you didn't, in fact, take a cigarette.'

'No. Because of the scream.'

'I beg your pardon?' Appleby looked at Miss Kentwell in astonishment.

'There was a scream, you see – from outside the house.

We heard it particularly clearly, because the window was open. So I –'

'One moment, Miss Kentwell. I suppose you have told Inspector Henderson about this scream?'

'Oh, no. He didn't ask me about it.'

'Good God, madam! How could he ask you about something he had no notion of? But no doubt Mr Ramsden –'

'Sir John, pray do not indulge in profanity. The matter was entirely trivial, but I am embarked upon a narrative of it, and will continue. The sound, I will own, startled me, and I moved over to the window to investigate.'

'That was most courageous of you.'

'Stuff and nonsense. I believe, however, that Mr Ramsden may have supposed something unpleasant to have occurred, since he made a motion to restrain me. However, we reached the window together, and realized how absurd was any apprehension we might have entertained.'

'I am relieved to hear it.'

'On the terrace directly below – as you will have noticed, if you have glanced out – there is a statue.'

'Hermes, Miss Kentwell. He conducts the souls of the dead to Hades, and is therefore designated *psuchopompos* by the ancient Greeks. An appropriate divinity for you to observe. But continue.'

'There is hardly anything more to tell. In that clear moonlight, all was apparent at once. The scream had come from a peacock, perched on the statue's head.'

'I've seen him there myself.' Appleby, if disappointed, was at least amused by this anticlimax. 'So here you are recalling an incident lasting no more than perhaps a couple of minutes. You propose to take a cigarette; are diverted by this alarming scream; and discover it to be, so to speak, a peacock's nest. What then?'

'I believe, Sir John, that it was immediately thereafter

that I came to reflect that I was not in what might formally be styled one of the reception-rooms of the house. A study, or the like, is prescriptively not so regarded. Of course Mr Ramsden had behaved with complete propriety in taking me there. We were seeking Mr Tytherton – and Mr Ramsden himself has clearly been entirely free of the establishment, and on a footing of perfect social equality with the Tythertons.'

'Clearly.' Appleby was very willing to accept these social niceties. 'So what?'

'I suggested to Mr Ramsden that we go on our way. And so we did.'

'Thank you very much. You have told me something that I find extremely interesting. I suppose you didn't see or hear the peacock again?'

'As I have just explained, we left the room at once.'

'Quite so. But what I have in mind is your return to it. In the interval Tytherton had been shot. And you were, I believe, in the room for some little time, attended by Mrs Catmull.'

'An absurd woman. Yes, that is so.'

'No further sight or sound of the peacock?'

'Definitely not. But I hardly see –'

'It isn't absolutely certain – is it? – that Tytherton was shot in that room, more or less as he sat at his desk. Just conceivably, his dead body may have been dragged there. But if a shot *was* fired there, close to the open window, I'd rather expect that peacock to make himself scarce for the rest of the night.'

'That, no doubt, is what is called detection.' Rather alarmingly, there was a faint hint of irony in Miss Kentwell's voice.

'I don't know that it's more than common sense.' Appleby, who had been sitting beside Miss Kentwell in quite a companionable way, stood up. 'And now I must continue my search for Mr Archie Tytherton. I wonder whether you have any observations to offer on that young man?'

Miss Kentwell considered.

'I can imagine,' she said, 'circumstances in which I should entertain high expectations of him.'

'Quite so.' And Appleby and Miss Kentwell exchanged what might fairly have been described as a meaningful glance. Only Appleby, as he walked away, found himself wondering whether this notable lady would find the slightest difficulty in rising to the boldest double bluff.

19

But the quest for Archie was again abortive for a time.
Outside the library, Appleby ran into Raffaello.

'I have,' Raffaello said.

'I beg your pardon?'

'Thought it over.' Raffaello glanced around him uneasily.
'Sir John, you are a man of discretion. We might perhaps
have a quiet conversation, away from your Inspector Henderson, don't you think? Come outside. It is pleasantly
warm on the terrace still. And here is a french window
we can slip through.'

'Very well. But you mustn't think I am going to enter
into a conspiracy with you.'

'Certainly not. Nothing of the kind.' Raffaello followed
Appleby into the open air. 'But I know you take a broad
view of this matter. Your only concern is with the shocking murder of Tytherton.'

'Understand clearly that my concern is with the law. But
it remains true that you will be wise to explain yourself,
Raffaello. And I think you want to begin with what was
supposed to be a robbery a couple of years ago.'

'It can be put that way – but only very unfairly, Sir
John. I had been out of the country, you see, and had
heard nothing about any disappearance of pictures from
Elvedon. It all seemed quite legitimate. Otherwise, I would
in no circumstances –'

'Tell your story, and don't waste time talking nonsense.'

'Very well.' Raffaello sighed like a man much ill-used. 'The late Mr Tytherton called on me, and we had a confidential discussion. He had a number of pictures of which he wished to dispose – quite unobtrusively, you understand. I agreed to put inquiries in hand.'

'Did he say anything about the background of this proposed quiet transaction?'

'I did form an opinion, Sir John.' Raffaello had now drawn his companion into a dignified perambulation of the splendid terrace of Elvedon. An uninstructed observer – Appleby thought – might have taken them for two Ministers of the Crown, gravely deliberating affairs of state. 'It was my business to satisfy myself of the propriety of what was being proposed. From, that is to say, an ethical point of view. So I did think about the matter. My conclusion was that Mr Tytherton felt rather in need of ready cash.'

'That sounds plausible. In the last year or so, at least, he is known to have been rather hard up.'

'Just so, Sir John.' Raffaello paused. He might have been calculating how much he was going to get away with, and soberly concluding it was likely to be very little. 'But another matter came up. I must be frank with you.'

'I'm afraid you must. And I suggest this to you, Raffaello. Whether you had been abroad or not, you knew perfectly well that the pictures Tytherton was proposing to part with were those that had already disappeared from Elvedon as the result of a faked robbery shortly before. Tytherton had already collected money on them from an insurance company, and now he was going to collect it all over again from your clients. Perhaps he really was desperately in need of money, or perhaps he just enjoyed dishonesty for its own sake. I rather suspect a mixture of the two. Well, however that may be, you tumbled to the situation. He couldn't really have had much expectation that you would not. You then told him that, if you were to play ball with him, there would have to be rather more in it for you. Whereupon he let you into some further plan or plot that was in his head. Am I right?'

'You put these things very unfairly – as I've already said.' Raffaello was once more a man aggrieved. 'I did gather that Tytherton intended to apply any money I could get him – or a good part of it – to another deal in the same field.'

'To *buying* pictures, you mean?'

'Something of the kind. He was in a position to make a very advantageous purchase. But of a highly confidential kind. It needed money. But nothing like the money it would finally bring in.' Raffaello paused. 'So we came to a gentleman's agreement in the matter. I was to act as his agent when the moment came to market this asset he was acquiring.'

'I see – and a precious pair of scoundrels you were. But go on.'

'There is really nothing more to tell you, Sir John.'

'Nonsense! Why are you here now?'

'Well, that moment had come – or was coming. *That* is why I am here. But Tytherton was evasive with me – very evasive indeed. He simply would not tell me what was in question. Imagine that, Sir John! I am very sorry to say anything harsh about a dead man. But I really don't think that Maurice Tytherton meant to be quite honest with me in the affair.'

'You shock and surprise me. And that was the position up to the moment of Tytherton's being killed?'

'Yes.'

'Then let us go back a little. How did the pictures you were quietly to dispose of two years ago come to you?'

'Come to me?' As he echoed the question, Raffaello glanced furtively round the long, deserted terrace. 'His nephew delivered them to me. Archie Tytherton.'

'The devil he did!' Appleby had paused beside that statue of the god Hermes upon which one of Elvedon's peacocks was accustomed to perch – a habit, he observed, of which there was humble evidence in the bespattered condition both of the divinity and his pedestal. And now Appleby leant against the adjacent balustrade and thoughtfully surveyed the splendours of the mansion itself. 'Did the young man know what he was about?'

'Ah! That is a question.'

'How can it be a question?'

'The pictures had been crated, Sir John. Each was in an individual light crate. Tytherton – this nephew, I mean – simply brought them up to town in an estate-car, and handed them over to my people at the gallery.'

'So he may have known much or little?'

'Or nothing at all. He was simply delivering to a highly reputable firm –'

'Quite so. And, now, one final question for the moment. You had better answer it honestly. Have you, up to this present minute and as a result of all the prowling round the house that you are known to have been doing, arrived at any notion at all as to what Maurice Tytherton had in some clandestine manner acquired and was presently proposing to profit from?'

'I have not!' Articulating this with some vehemence, Raffaello further pointed his feelings by a gesture like a savage brandishing of the fist before the impassive face of Elvedon Court. 'Do you know what, Sir John? I am coming to believe that I have been the victim of an unscrupulous imposture. I am deeply sorry to say it.

But Maurice Tytherton was little better than a blackguard.'

At this edifying moment there was an interruption. Mark Tytherton had stepped abruptly from the house, with the result that Raffaello's threatening gesticulation took on the appearance of having been directed at him. And Mark's reaction was not of the most temperate sort.

'It's you again, is it?' he demanded, and took three long steps forward. 'And did I hear you say something about my father?'

'Nothing of the kind!' Raffaello – not unreasonably, considering the physical indignity to which he had already been subjected by this violent young man earlier in the day – was terrified. 'I assure you –'

'You assure me you are a beastly toad.' Despite Appleby's restraining presence, Mark took a further menacing step forward. 'Isn't that right?'

'Yes, certainly. I agree. Anything!' All dignity had forsaken the unfortunate art dealer. He began cautiously to back away down the terrace.

'Sir John,' Mark Tytherton demanded, 'are the police finished with this man?'

'I judge it improbable. Although not in the sense that they will insist on his staying here.'

'Then you can clear out.' Mark had turned to Raffaello. 'First thing after breakfast.'

'I'll go now.'

'You'll go when I say – at ten o'clock tomorrow morning. You were my father's guest, and you'll end your connection with the place at decent notice. But get off this terrace. I don't like you.' For some moments Mark's eye brooded over Raffaello's precipitate retreat, and then he turned to Appleby. 'Well,' he asked, 'did Henderson tell you?'

'About your interview with your father last night? Certainly.'

'Do you think they'll lock me up?'

'Let us not pursue that for the moment. And, even if they do, you'll have a bit of a run for your money, Mark.'

'What do you mean by that, sir?' The young man looked sharply at Appleby, very aware of this use of his Christian name.

'As master of Elvedon. Who else are you going to order off the premises – Ronnie Ramsden?'

'Yes, of course – all in due time. You don't imagine, do you, I need a chap to manage a home farm and some tenants for me?'

'I don't think I do. By the way, I gather Ramsden and you were at school together. What was he like?'

'Brutal.'

'Was he brutal to you?'

'He didn't have the chance. We became prefects together. But then he was given the top job, and ran the place. I'll give it to him that he did it damned well. The school was a slack dump when he became head boy, and he sorted it out extremely efficiently.'

'But not gently?'

'Not gently at all.'

'And you sound as if you disapproved, Mark. Didn't you throw your weight about a bit yourself? You seem to me a little given to –'

'Not like that.' Mark Tytherton produced what was suddenly a disarming grin. 'I never thought much of morale-building with a stick. Still, the stick-merchants have something. It can be done.'

'Yes, it can be done.' Appleby accepted this mature view of things soberly. 'Incidentally, do you think there would be any gentler way of building a little morale into that cousin of yours?'

'Archie? I'm sure there wouldn't. He's in a disgusting funk – isn't he? I've no use for Master Archie Tytherton. Out he goes, double quick.'

'You don't feel that might be a little – well, brutal?'

'Lord, no! My father will have left him something. Archie has a kind of legitimate vested interest as a parasite. But he can go off and enjoy the status elsewhere. I don't want to see him again.'

'As it happens, I do. Do you by any chance know where I can find him now?'

'I haven't a clue. But here's the omniscient Ronnie Ramsden, who always has tabs on everything. Ask him.'

Ramsden had indeed appeared on the terrace, and was now pausing before them. It wasn't, clearly, a chance encounter. Ramsden had something to say to one or other of them. It turned out to be Appleby.

'I have a message from Colonel Pride,' he said. 'He has been called away for some urgent reason or other. But one of his men will keep a car at your disposal until he returns.'

'Thank you. I'll have it take me home in an hour's time, or thereabouts. My wife won't be pleased if I'm late for dinner.'

'I'll give her a message to that effect.' Ramsden looked at Appleby curiously. 'Shall you be coming back tomorrow?'

'Oh, later tonight, quite possibly. I'm sure everybody wants this affair cleared up as soon as may be.'

'And that's what you're going to do?'

'I judge it probable.'

'Well, I shall be much relieved, for one.' Ramsden had glanced quickly at Mark Tytherton, as if wondering how he had been struck by the attitude of this cock-sure retired policeman. But he spoke unaffectedly enough. 'We're not a comfortable or agreeable household. The sooner we're sorted out, the better pleased Mark is likely to be. Isn't that so, Mark? And, of course, your step-mother.'

'I'll thank you, Ronnie, not to go on calling Alice that.'

'My dear man, I'll call her whatever you please. You're the boss.' Ramsden said this without irony or resentment; it was as if he acknowledged it as being in the nature of the situation that his own status had changed, and was perfectly willing amicably to pack his bag when asked. And this good humour had an effect on Mark.

'Ronnie, I was saying you're the chap who has tabs on everything. I expect you've been doing quite a job. Just at this moment, do you happen to know where Archie is? Sir John wants to have a go at him.'

'A go at him?' Ramsden smiled grimly. 'Why, the poor devil's dead scared already. I don't know what he'll be like when the big guns are brought to bear. Still, it's his own messy fault.'

'I wonder,' Appleby asked, 'if you would elaborate on that judgement?'

'I suppose I could, sir.' Ramsden again glanced at Mark, but this time uncomfortably. 'Only, Mr Tytherton's just dead, and Mark's just home –'

'Ronnie, stop parading nice feelings. They're not your line.' Mark spoke roughly. 'And everybody knows Elvedon has been a pigsty for quite some time. So get on with it.'

'Very well.' Ramsden had flushed faintly. 'Your father found Archie in bed with somebody, and very much disapproved. There was –'

'With Alice, you mean?'

'Of course not. With that awful woman Cynthia Graves. There was a revolting row –'

'When was this?'

'Don't be so thick, Mark.' Ramsden was suddenly impatient. 'You know perfectly well. It happened only yesterday. And your father rang up his solicitor, intending to bash Archie out of his will. And then it was your father who got bashed – fatally. So Archie's panic at least has a rational basis. Like almost everybody else in Elvedon, he's in an awkward spot.' Ramsden had directed one of his swift glances at Appleby. 'Only other people keep a slightly stiffer upper lip.'

'What you insisted on kids doing when you took that stick to them,' Mark said.

'What on earth are you talking about?'

'Oh, never mind. Sir John's question is, what has become of Archie now. Have you any notion?'

'I have, as a matter of fact. About a quarter of an hour ago, I saw him slinking off across the park.'

'Ah!' Appleby said. 'Then I will take a walk there myself. And I'll be glad of your company.'

'Both of us?' Ramsden asked.

'Yes, if you will be so good. I'm rather tired of têtes-à-têtes. I've a notion that a little committee-work might advance matters now.'

20

But their first encounter was with Mr Voysey. He rose up suddenly before them, like a clerical triton, from amid a green sea of mare's-tails.

'Ah, good afternoon,' he said, and made a vaguely benignant gesture with what proved to be a pair of field-glasses. 'I think I have just spotted a lesser whitethroat. One frequently hears – does one not? – that flat little rattle from thick cover. But actual observation is another matter. However, I scarcely think I can have been mistaken. There was that small dark patch behind the eye.' Having concluded these ornithological remarks, Voysey appeared to notice Mark Tytherton for the first time. 'My dear Mark,' he said, 'I am glad to see you. But I fear you have had a sad welcome home. You will have everybody's sympathy. And we must remember –' The vicar checked himself, apparently judging the moment inapposite for the more formal comforts of religion. 'Perhaps we may have a talk one day soon.'

'Perhaps we may. I believe it is through a hole in a little glass window. This is Sir John Appleby –'

'I have already met Sir John.'

'– and he is going to put either Ronnie or me in gaol. Or perhaps Archie, unless he opts for Catmull instead. Or you, for that matter.' Having decided to exercise his wit in this acrid way, Mark went at it with a will. 'Incidentally, I'm not confident you are right about that lesser whitethroat. I even think you may be getting a little hazy about your species. Didn't you mistake me for a badger only last night?'

'Stop being stupid, Mark.' Ronnie Ramsden said this with the precise degree of authority proper in the captain of a school towards a fellow prefect. 'And what's this about last night?'

'I was prowling around. I came into the house. I saw my father and had a row with him. What you might call a terminal row. I thought everybody knew by now. The police do.'

'I see.' Ramsden said this so quietly that Appleby saw the information had startled him. But their encounter with the vicar appeared to be a mere marking time, and there had been enough of that. So Appleby intervened.

'We are looking for Archie Tytherton,' he said briskly. 'He's thought to be walking in the park. You don't happen to have seen him?'

'Yes, I have. And he was in my mind only a moment ago, when Mark said something about badgers, the sense of which escaped me. Archie has never mentioned the fact to me, but I believe he must be interested in badgers himself.'

'I'd have expected him to stick to bipeds,' Mark said. 'But, of course, one never knows.'

'Restrain yourself,' Mr Voysey said, with sudden and surprising severity. 'You are in the company of two people much older than yourself.'

'Sorry, padre.' Mark Tytherton – Appleby had remarked before – did quite well when rebuked. 'Tell us about Archie.'

'Only seconds before you came up with me, I happened to turn my glasses on the spinney in Low Coomb. You know there are several setts there?'

'Of course.' Mark was impatient. 'They've been there for hundreds of years. The whole coomb is a maze of the things. I knew it very well when I was a kid.'

'Quite so. And you can see something of the nearest sett with the naked eye now. Archie Tytherton was examining it closely.'

'Archie was turning to natural history?' Ramsden was sharply incredulous. 'And this afternoon, when he's in a blue funk?'

'I could not possibly be mistaken. I trained these binoculars on him. He was on his hands and knees, peering down into the sett. And this was not ten minutes ago.'

'Then he must be in the spinney, or on the path leading from it, now.' Ramsden turned to Appleby. 'Shall we walk across to it?'

'Certainly.' And with no more than a gesture to the vicar, Appleby stepped out at once. 'Do you know,' he said to Mark, 'that I believe your cousin is going to have the small distinction of satisfying what may be pretty well my last curiosity in this affair?'

'So much the better.' It was observable that a certain confidence, hitherto lacking, had come to Mark Tytherton. 'You clear up the mystery of my father's death, and I'll turn a stiff spot of spit-and-polish on Elvedon in general.' He turned cheerfully to Ramsden. 'What you bloody well did at school,' he said. 'My turn now.'

In a couple of minutes Archie Tytherton had come into view. He had very little the appearance of one at ease amid the beautiful and permanent forms of nature. He was scurrying along in the manner of something that has been disturbed under a stone.

'Like one,' Appleby said, 'that on a lonesome road doth walk in fear and dread.'

'Precisely.' Ramsden laughed softly. 'Because he knows a frightful fiend doth close behind him tread.'

'It's no sight to prompt poetical effusion.' Mark seemed to offer this reproof seriously. 'The poor chap's funk is bluer still. As blue as a baboon's behind. And you won't find *that* in *The Ancient Mariner* ... He's spotted us. I think he's going to bolt.'

This, however, didn't happen – perhaps for no better reason than that there was nowhere very useful to bolt to. Although in a wavering fashion, Archie came on. And he halted when he had to, which was when Appleby and the two young men barred his way. There was a moment's unkind silence.

'Oh, hullo,' Archie said in a surprised tone, as if it were only in this instant that he had noticed them.

'Oh, hullo, you squalid little brute,' Mark said with a plunge into his most juvenile manner. 'This is Sir John Appleby. He hoped for a word with you while you munched your bun in the tea-break. But you bolted for the wide open spaces. And apparently to muck in with the badgers.'

'The badgers?' For a moment Archie was blank. 'Oh, yes. I've been reading a book about them.'

'Whose book?'

'How should I know? It's a green book, but with a kind of yellow-green cover.'

'You shocking little –'

'Perhaps,' Appleby interrupted, 'I may have my word with Mr Tytherton now? Mr Tytherton, you have in fact just been observing the habits of these interesting creatures in what is called, I believe, Low Coomb?'

'I don't see how you can –'

'Old Voysey,' Mark said, 'with a pair of field-glasses. I-God-see-you kind of thing.'

'Mark, please be quiet.' Appleby had raised a mildly restraining hand. 'Do I understand, Mr Tytherton, that your reading in the green book has prompted you to believe that badgers are to be seen gambolling around in daylight?'

'Must be fair,' Mark said. 'Does sometimes happen. But it's damned uncommon.'

'Shut up, Mark.' Ramsden's easy authority was suddenly tinged with annoyance, or something more. 'You're too bloody fond of the sound of your own voice. Save it up. It will sound splendid in a deserted Elvedon.'

'Will you two gentlemen,' Appleby said, 'be good enough to let me continue my conversation with Mr Tytherton? Perhaps, Mr Tytherton, on this occasion your interest was simply in the appearance of the setts?'

'The setts? Oh, yes – of course. That was it. Pad marks and dung pits. And they put out their bedding to air.'

'And all these interesting appearances are on view in Low Coomb?'

'Oh, yes.' Archie Tytherton nodded vigorously. 'Everything the book says.'

'Perhaps you won't mind turning back and showing me. I am myself a keen naturalist. And I believe that both your cousin and Mr Ramsden will find a good deal of curiosity in what we are going to see.'

'I really don't think –'

'March, Archie.' Mark Tytherton was peremptory. 'Or *be* marched. Which won't be comfortable.'

Thus under threat of outrageous compulsion, Archie looked despairingly around him. He was a plump and flabby youth, somewhat undersized, and neither in physique nor by temperament likely to put up a good show. Appleby, who would have been indisposed to lend countenance to violence, hoped that intimidation (equally reprehensible, but less easy to prove before a magistrate) would suffice. And it did. Archie turned round and moved off reluctantly in his former tracks.

'Round this side,' Archie said.

'I think not, Mr Tytherton. Your recollection is at fault – for here are your footprints in the grass. Your cousin, who was certainly a Boy Scout in his time, will support me.'

'Quite right,' Mark said. 'We go this way. But I wasn't a Scout for very long. They poured water down my sleeve for no better reason than that I called them bloody little bastards. So I quit.'

'But it *isn't* that way! I came *this* way – and over to *that* sett.' Archie had halted with the stubbornness of despair. 'And I *won't* be marched.'

'Mr Tytherton, perhaps we have had enough of this nonsense.' Appleby was walking on. 'If we don't find what we are looking for now, I can have this whole coomb dug up by noon tomorrow. The badgers won't be pleased – nor the police either. So have some sense.'

'I don't know what –'

'Mr Tytherton, try the truth. It's what I go round Elvedon recommending. It can be very liberating, the truth. Literally so. Have a stab at it, and it's conceivable you'll have a chance of staying out of gaol. I don't put it higher than that. Just a chance.'

'All right, all right,' Archie said. 'I only took them because I wanted to give them to Mark. Everybody knows they belong to him.'

'What the devil are you talking about, you little rat?' Mark had seized his cousin, not amicably, by the collar.

'You let go!' Archie produced this as a squeal. 'If you assault me, you filthy great oaf, Sir John What's-His-Name will have to be a witness.'

'It's a colourable reason for having taken them,' Appleby said. 'But what then?'

'I suppose I got a bit scared.'

'A bit scared!' Mark was contemptuous. 'Why, you've been sweating your bags off, you poor sot, all day. Your nerve would crumble, if you'd pinched a bag of sweets from a four-year-old.'

'Mark, keep your reading of character for another occasion.' Appleby turned to Archie. 'Fish them out, please – from whichever of these holes you've hidden them in.'

This part of the coomb bore an odd resemblance, on a Lilliputian scale, to a derelict industrial landscape. Everywhere spreading deposits of earth, part-overgrown with nettles and elders, suggested extensive mining operations for the most part abandoned long ago. It would have been possible to count at least a dozen major entrances to what were doubtless the commodious, if often untenanted, mansions within. A large rabbit-warren could not have been a more suitable place for what had been Archie Tytherton's purpose; and what he had hidden, it might have taken much digging to reveal. But Archie had knelt down, and thrust his arm into a cavity. He straightened up, and shoved a small, untidily wrapped parcel into Appleby's hands.

'There you damned well are,' he cried – with a sudden viciousness momentarily overcoming his terror. 'And much good may they do anyone.'

'Thank you.' Appleby undid the parcel and opened the jewel-case. *'Une parure de diamants,'* he said, snapped the case shut again, and handed it to Mark Tytherton. 'I don't recommend ever attaching massive sentimental associations to such things. It only leads to trouble – as I think your recent experience must constrain you to agree. Mr Ramsden, have you anything useful to say about this?'

'Nothing whatever.' Ramsden had started upon being addressed. He was staring at Archie fixedly. 'You ought to be prosecuted and sent to prison,' he said coldly. 'But I suppose the very circumstance that makes your theft most disgusting – its being a family affair – will save your beastly skin. Mark won't prosecute.'

'That is not quite the position.' Appleby was grim. 'It's for the police to decide whether to prosecute this young man. And, if they do, it will take a hazardous amount of perjury on Mark's part to get him off. However, that's for the future. At the moment, I think Mr Tytherton has a certain amount to tell me. So we'll say that the committee now breaks up. I'll walk back to the house with him, and leave you two to have your own amicable chat.'

'We're not enemies,' Ramsden said easily. 'Or are we, Mark?'

'We're old acquaintances.' Mark turned abruptly to Appleby. 'I hope,' he said with an odd formality, 'you'll dine at Elvedon?'

'Thank you, but no. I must go home to Dream.'

'To dream, sir?' Mark was perplexed.

'A house called Long Dream. It's where I live.'

21

'The Chief Constable was most apologetic,' Inspector Henderson was saying to Appleby half an hour later. 'He thought it uncivil to go off without a word to you. Particularly as he can't get back. An impromptu royal visit somewhere – and he works it all out himself. A very conscientious man, Colonel Pride.' Henderson opened the door of his car. 'I thought that, if you'd let me drive you home myself, we might have a kind of conference on the way.'

'We can certainly have a conference. But I'm not going home, as a matter of fact. So draw up just on the other side of that imposing bridge.'

'Very good, sir.' Henderson asked no question. He was a man wholly at ease in a hierarchical system.

'I've absolutely broadcast the fact that I'm going home. What I actually propose is to walk quietly back to the house and take another leisured look round. Dinner will be keeping everybody busy – even Catmull at table and Mrs Catmull in her kitchen. Have you left any men in Elvedon yourself?'

'Two, just at the moment. To keep an unobtrusive eye on things, you might say.'

'Quite right. Will they keep an unobtrusive eye on me?'

'They know who you are pretty well, Sir John, and will carry out any instructions you give.'

'I'll only want them not to hold me up. But wait a minute. Will one of them have the key of Maurice Tytherton's workroom?'

'No, sir. It's in my pocket now.'

'Then I think I'll relieve you of it, just for the time being. Can you be back at Elvedon yourself by nine o'clock?'

'Yes, of course. Earlier, if you prefer it.'

'Nine will do. And I think you'd better have a few more men around. We'll call it the hour at which we begin to close in.'

'That's a very encouraging expression, Sir John.'

'Here we are.' They were running over the Palladian bridge. 'Stop on the other side, and we'll admire the view. And it won't take me ten minutes to tell you what tentative conclusions I've come to in this affair.'

The superannuations of sunk realms, Appleby told himself. This time, he had started at the top of the house, and wandered through a seemingly endless series of attic rooms. Some were small, and some very large. Some harboured nothing except dust and cobwebs. Others were piled to the roof with the kind of junk – often rather opulent-looking in an outmoded fashion – that accumulates over the generations in a large country house. Appleby wondered whether there had been a radical clearance when the first Tythertons took over Elvedon, or whether in a fabric so generous of elbow-room nobody had much bothered. The acquisitiveness of the English propertied classes – he reflected as, in one chamber, he peered into a jungle of abandoned iron and brass bedsteads – is evidenced in such places. They won't let anything go. Even when you know you will never have twenty indoor servants again, you don't send such humble amenities as you have hitherto allowed them to the scrap yard. You tell the remaining half-dozen to cart the stuff up to your lumber-rooms. No doubt there was something in it for the social historian. Suppose the whole of Elvedon to be suddenly buried under lava, and then excavated a thousand years on. A refined researcher, comparing what was down below with what had been banished to this obscure elevation, might be able to trace certain radical changes of taste in the course of the house's quite short history. Hip-baths: they had their date. But bird-cages – when had the English gentry gone in for caged birds in a big way? Appleby didn't know – but there was one room almost full of such contraptions. Perhaps one scholar, well-seen in such matters, would tumble to what might be called the Maurice Tytherton Revolution. Statues and busts heavy enough to threaten to fall through the floor, furniture which had enjoyed one spell of modishness or another, Regency frames without pictures and Victorian pictures without frames, tartan carpets which must have been imported by some Tytherton well affected to the dear Queen: there had certainly at some recent date been a wholesale banishing from public view at Elvedon of these and much else. No doubt Maurice Tytherton – that man of taste, as Tommy Pride had early certified him to be – had been responsible for much overturning of established nineteenth-century sanctities in his ancestral home.

As far as he was concerned, Appleby told himself, these attics were no go. The police search whole counties for buried bodies; airports and transatlantic liners for time-bombs; vast hotels for wads of forged bank-notes and packets of doubtful drugs. Quite frequently their efforts appear to be crowned with success, or so we are assured in newspapers. But even humble operations of this sort take time. Set a squad of men searching here for a specific object, or class of objects, and it might be days rather than hours before they produce results. Appleby dusted himself down, and descended to the next floor.

Here, however, he had done some exploring already, and his present visit would have struck a casual observer as somewhat perfunctory. He entered half a dozen rooms, furnished or empty, and peered absently into a few cupboards and through a few windows. He paced a corridor, whistling moodily the while. Then he checked himself, reflecting that, while the high ceremony of dinner was going on below, a certain amount of house-maiding might go on up here. The Italian girls interested him, but he didn't want to run into any of them just yet. It might be useful, however, to know how they came and went, and he gave a few minutes to finding the service staircase. Having descended it to the first floor, he went straight to the workroom. Elvedon, despite the high lucidity of its architecture, was rather easy to get lost in; nevertheless he was beginning to feel he could now get round it in the dark. He unlocked the door, entered, and closed it behind him.

Dusk was falling, and he switched on the lights. What his eye first fell on was Mark Tytherton's photograph, once so affectingly reported on by Miss Kentwell, which indeed stood in a silver frame on the dead man's writing-table. He picked it up and examined it curiously. What one would have expected, somehow, would have been the portrait of a schoolboy. But this was the portrait – was very much the portrait – of the young man Appleby knew. He frowned over this, turned the thing over, removed the back of the frame, and found himself looking at the gold-lettered name and address of a photographer in Buenos Aires. So no wonder Mark was the heir of Elvedon; the propensity his father and he had formed for quarrelling hadn't impaired the decent intercourse this recent gift testified to. Appleby spent a further moment or two peering rather closely at this piece of evidence, and then returned it to its place.

He stared at the floor and stared at the ceiling – rather as if expecting them to reveal trap-doors and spy-holes. He walked over to the Goya, and stared at that. Then – and he might have been a man overtaken by *folie de doute* – he reached up and passed a cautious finger over the *impasto* with which the painter had rendered the high-lights of this Spanish grandee's cravat. He shook his head, turned away, and made a final survey of the room at large. He nodded – much as a stage-manager might do when satisfied with his *mise en scène* – and then switched off the lights, left the room, and locked its door behind him. He glanced at his watch. It wasn't likely that the present ill-assorted company at Elvedon would much linger over their evening meal. But he still had at least fifteen minutes to himself. In that time, there were several matters upon which he would be glad to instruct himself. He made his way to the ground floor.

The door of Catmull's pantry was ajar. As once before, Appleby walked in.

'Oh, hullo!' he said. 'Why aren't you eating your nice dinner?'

'I pleaded a headache.'

'Ah – what is called a nervous headache, no doubt. You really ought a little to spare yourself. Incidentally, I should have expected the Catmulls to lock up when leaving their household goods unguarded.'

'They did. I've just picked the lock.' Miss Kentwell sounded mildly surprised, as if the fact might have been taken for granted.

'I see. Well, I'm afraid you must be called a most disingenuous lady. Would you still maintain that there might be circumstances in which you could entertain high expectations of our friend Archie Tytherton – as a co-respondent, or whatever?'

'I don't know why not, Sir John.' Miss Kentwell, who

had been studying one of Catmull's emaciated race-horses, now took the creature boldly from its hook, and placed it face-downwards on a table. 'In my trade one does occasionally kill two birds with one stone. Or affects to be after one bird, while really aiming at another.'

'This unfortunate dead man, Maurice Tytherton, really believed you to be here because he had retained you to spy out and document his wife's infidelities?'

'Most certainly. And so I was.'

'But also?'

'Well, it is perfectly true that my agency accepted what may be called a double-booking.' Miss Kentwell, although her ear was obviously alert for sounds in the corridor, smiled at Appleby, very much at her ease. Then she tapped the back of the heavy frame before her. 'And it can't be said that I haven't carried out my assignment. Just take a look, Sir John.'

Appleby took a look – and spent some minutes taking other looks.

'Well, well,' he said. 'Tell me, would it be *Novoexport*?'

'Yes, indeed. And I may say they are excellent employers. As for these things' – and Miss Kentwell made a gesture round the walls – 'they are undoubtedly the legal property of the government of the U.S.S.R.'

'Who send you chummy letters with nice stamps. And not in vain, since the stuff will now be returned to them.'

'Indeed it will. I shall have the pleasure of alerting that nice Inspector Henderson – and he will have the pleasure of being active in two *causes célèbres* at once. He will have quite a spin with Interpol, and his photograph will be in the papers.'

'I knew from the first that you were the most benevolent of women. I positively begin to believe in all that charitable zeal.' Appleby turned to the door. 'By the way, do your many accomplishments include fluent Italian?'

'I am afraid not.'

'A pity – then I must make do with my own. Henderson, incidentally, is going to summon a little gathering for nine o'clock.'

'Indeed, Sir John – and for what purpose?'

'A short conference over Tytherton's death. I think it fair that everybody should know exactly how it came about.'

'Which is something that *you* know?'

'Oh, certainly, Miss Kentwell. I have all the facts. But I rather hope to find a further scrap or two of evidence.'

'And these?' Miss Kentwell again pointed to Catmull's picture gallery. 'These are another story?'

'Almost.' Appleby laughed – briefly and grimly. 'But not quite.'

'*Buona sera, signorina,*' Appleby said – quite confidently, so far.

'*Buona sera, signor.*' The Italian girl – and this was the prettiest of them, Appleby thought – was a shade startled by the sudden appearance of a gentleman in this obscure corner of Elvedon's domestic offices. But she wasn't disapproving. She probably had rather a dull life. Archie Tytherton had doubtless made improper advances to her, but there surely couldn't be much fun in that. And at least she wasn't supposing that Appleby was on that kind of prowl himself. She was looking puzzled and expectant, but innocent enough.

'*Come vi chiamate?*' Appleby asked paternally.

'*Mi chiamo Annunziata, signor.*'

'*Bene!*' Appleby received this information with grave approval. '*Per favore, Annunziata, dove sono i rifiuti?*'

'*Signor?*' It was perhaps the oddity rather than the

obscurity of this question that bewildered Annunziata. And in his quest of domestic litter Appleby now threw in everything he had.

'*I cestini dei rifiuti,*' he said, '*e della carta straccia. Mi capite? La cartàccia.*' He paused. '*Carta da gettare nei rifiuti?*' he produced as a final variant. '*Dove?*'

'*Suvvia!*' Annunziata smiled brilliantly. However eccentric these demands, she had understood them. '*Andiamo!*' she amplified. And she led Appleby into regions of Elvedon yet more humble and obscure.

22

'It is very good of you all to have come together in this way,' Appleby said. 'Particularly as for some of you, as for myself, it's a matter of standing-room only. The late Mr Tytherton didn't intend this room for large companies, and the furnishing is a little inadequate to our present purposes. However, it will not be necessary to detain you long.'

Nine o'clock had sounded on the stable clock, and the round-up had been brought about in the workroom. Mark Tytherton, with what was perhaps an unconscious assumption of proprietorship, had sat down behind his father's writing-table. Alice Tytherton and Mrs Graves were perched together – most inappropriately – on the Italian *cassone*. Miss Kentwell was on a low chair in front of the window, occupied with her embroidery. The only other comfortable chairs had been appropriated by Carter and Raffaello. Archie Tytherton was sitting cross-legged on the floor – perhaps from an obscure feeling that he might get off more lightly if he looked as much as possible like a small boy. Ramsden was leaning against the door. Catmull was standing in one corner of the room (it would not have been proper for him to sit down, anyway), and Inspector Henderson in another. Mrs Catmull had been excused these curious proceedings. And Sir John Appleby stood in front of the fireplace, with Goya's nobleman above his head. It was now an hour after sunset, and almost dark outside. But the evening was warm, and the window had been left open and the curtains undrawn. When the moon rose it would be a beautiful night.

'Some of you may be a little puzzled,' Appleby began, 'why I myself am here at all. It simply happened that my friend Colonel Pride brought me over this morning for the purpose of introducing me to Mr Tytherton. There was some idea that I might be consulted, I think. Certainly, when I heard that a number of valuable paintings had disappeared from Elvedon a couple of years ago, it occurred to me that Mr Tytherton might have it in mind to ask me whether I thought any useful steps could still be taken to effect their recovery. It is a matter, I should explain, of which I have experience. The first supposition of mine, however, has proved to be wrong.'

'Do you mean, Sir John,' Ramsden asked, 'that there was, in fact, no intention to tap your professional knowledge?'

'I don't mean that, either – and I think I began guessing as much when I became aware of the presence at Elvedon of Mr Raffaello. He too, in his way, is a man of special experience in such matters.'

'You be careful what you say,' Raffaello interrupted rudely. 'There are a lot of people here – and there's such a thing as the law of slander.'

'Mr Raffaello is perfectly right. He just hasn't been given a chance to get going at Elvedon, and must be accounted blameless at least in the immediate context I am considering. Shocking though it may seem, Mr Tytherton, although he had trusted Mr Raffaello in an interesting transaction a couple of years ago, he didn't quite trust him on the present occasion. But I must not talk in riddles. Let me simply say that picture-dealing – to give it a polite name – is prominent in this affair. Mr Tytherton had a big, and totally illegal, operation to put through; he thought of employing Raffaello – now, as he had done before; but he had a notion of picking my brains about the shady side of the thing in general. So, incidentally, at a later stage and somewhat naively, had our friend Catmull here.'

'Nothing of the kind!' Catmull broke in robustly. 'In a position of trust, I was. And can prove it.'

'In a limited sense, that will presently prove to be true.' Appleby paused. 'I have been led to place this matter of picture-dealing and picture-stealing in the forefront of the thing, and I am afraid you will have to listen to a little more about them later. But now –'

'Can't you stick to what is plainly at the heart of the affair?' It was Charles Carter who asked this, and with an air of simple impatience. 'If crooked art-deals were the occasion of Tytherton's death –'

'I understand Mr Carter's anxiety to exclude from these public explanations extraneous matters which may possibly be of an unedifying sort.' Appleby spoke without irony. 'And we need not, I believe, positively dig in them. But the circumstances of the case are so complex that I fear I cannot be over-nice about it all. And now let me go on. Mr Carter will perhaps allow me to be sufficiently relevant if I begin with the finding of the body. This is supposed to have been by Mr Ramsden and Miss Kentwell round about –'

'Supposed?' Ramsden queried sharply.

'Round about eleven-twenty. In fact, it was discovered by Mr Archie Tytherton, and at a somewhat earlier hour.' Appleby paused. 'Perhaps a significantly earlier hour. But now, I fear, I have to go back a little, and to touch upon certain matters of just the sort Mr Carter has been deprecating any airing of. Earlier yesterday, the late Mr Tytherton and his nephew had a sharp quarrel – I will merely say over something that reflected singularly little credit on either of them. And it had nothing to do with pictures.'

'It seems to have had something to do with jewels,' Mark said grimly.

'Not really. That is a theme I have to come to a little later.'

'But might we at least say,' Ramsden asked acridly, 'that their quarrel was about a pearl among women?'

'Is that me?' Mrs Graves asked and looked round the company as one conscious that a compliment has been paid to her. 'Not that it is at all refined to be quarrelled over by gentlemen.'

'Sir John,' Miss Kentwell said authoritatively, 'be pleased to proceed.'

'Very well. His dispute with his uncle upset Mr Archie Tytherton very much – particularly when he heard that his uncle had sent for his solicitor. Mr Archie, I understand, cannot in any sense be described as gainfully employed. He had an allowance from his uncle; he looked for a legacy from his uncle; so here was the writing on the wall. His response to this crisis in his affairs was to get very tolerably drunk. Mr Tytherton, that was so?'

'That's right.' Archie nodded nervously and eagerly. 'Most awfully, really. Not responsible for myself, and all that, for the rest of the evening.'

'A judge might conceivably give some slight weight to such a contention. It was in this state of inebriety, however, that Mr Archie achieved what must be called, I fear, his only rational action in the course of the affair. When he knew that his uncle had withdrawn to this room, he resolved to come and plead with him.'

'You'd jolly well have done the same thing yourself,' Archie said, still from his juvenile stance on the floor. He appeared not to appreciate that a mild commendation had been offered him. 'If they'd been going to turn *you* away without a bloody bean.'

'It took the young man quite some time,' Appleby continued, 'actually to nerve himself to come along. But eventually he did so. It was to find that his uncle had been shot dead.'

'Do we just have Archie's word for that?' Ramsden asked.

'Yes, Mr Ramsden – simply Archie's word. And we have only Archie's word, too, for how he then comported himself. As it may be said, however, to transcend imagination, I think we may place reasonable reliance upon it. Mr Archie Tytherton did a rummage. The expression is his own. And I have no doubt he will be happy to confirm it now.'

'That's right,' Archie said promptly. 'The old boy being shot was, of course, an awful shock, and all that. Still, a quick rummage seemed the thing.'

'In the course of this hopeful exercise, it appears that Mr Archie opened a drawer in that writing-table which may be described as having been virtually under the dead man's nose. He found a jewel-case, opened it, and knew what was there at once. They were diamond ornaments, and for the moment I will describe them merely as an heirloom which had been moving to and fro a good deal between what may be termed the ladies of this establishment.'

'Maurice told me he had sold them.' Alice Tytherton said this perfectly calmly, and followed up her words by giving Mrs Graves, perched beside her, a cold and equally calm stare. 'I knew he was a liar, I need hardly say.'

'So Mr Archie Tytherton pocketed the things, and made off to his room. He spent some minutes trying to decide where to hide them for the night. Then – already very frightened, I think – he undressed and got into bed. He says the stable clock was striking eleven.' Appleby looked contemplatively for a moment at the hero of this recital. 'His only further positive achievement was to think up a purposeless cock-and-bull story about a nightmare. At the moment he is a little sustained by being the centre of your attention, but in the main he now exists in a condition of abject terror. For is it not very colourable, as Mr Ramsden has hinted, that his earlier account of himself has been a cock-and-bull affair too? May he not have shot his uncle himself? He had a very good motive in the preventing his uncle from making a new will. But then – to put it with necessary brutality – so too did his uncle's friend Mrs Graves.'

'That's right,' Archie said. 'I'll bet it was her. Funny I hadn't thought of it.'

'Mr Tytherton, you may spare us your further remarks. And I now pass to another matter. I move back in time – from Mr Archie Tytherton's concerns to those of his cousin, Mr Mark Tytherton.'

'That's fine by me,' Mark interjected. 'And I do think we've had enough of Archie.'

'Seconded and carried,' Ramsden said.

'Mark Tytherton returned from overseas a few days ago, and put up in a local inn. For family reasons of a delicate nature, he hesitated to come to Elvedon. Last night, however, he eventually did so, entering the house, unobserved, just after ten o'clock. It was the hour at which his father, even if entertaining guests, commonly came up here for a while. Knowing this, Mark walked straight upstairs to this room.'

'All this is just my story,' Mark said composedly.

'Certainly it is – but let me take it at its face value for the time being. Father and son meet in decent amity, and

186

have a drink. Unfortunately Mark rather hastily advances a subject that rankles with him; even obsesses him at times, it is fair to say. And here we are back with the diamonds. They had been the property of Mark's mother, Maurice Tytherton's first wife. Mark is aware of what must be called certain moral weaknesses in his father's character, and he is convinced that the jewels are now in the possession of Mrs Graves, who may be described as for the time being his father's intimate friend. So there is a sudden quarrel – as is the fashion, one may be tempted to think, in this unfortunate household. Maurice Tytherton declines to act in the matter, and Mark, still unobserved, flings out of the house in a rage. He has been in it for only fifteen minutes.'

'It may all be a fairy-story,' Mark said.

'Of course it may. But now I have the kind testimony of Mrs Graves. She had indeed been in the enjoyment of the diamonds for some time; and this may, or may not, have been admitted by Maurice Tytherton in his interview with his son last night. Certainly this morning Mark Tytherton, having come to Elvedon to condole with his step-mother, ran into Mrs Graves and taxed her in the matter – speaking to her, I fear, most violently and improperly. Mrs Graves denied having possession of the jewels, and later in the morning she made her way to his inn, the Hanged Man, to reiterate this denial, and perhaps explain herself. But Mark was quickly in a rage again, and in fact I myself interrupted another useless and uninformative quarrel. I was much at fault, as it happens, in not getting a little more out of Mrs Graves there and then. But the actual course of events is at least perfectly clear now.'

'It's far from clear to me,' Charles Carter said.

'My dear sir, simply consider. Mrs Graves has had this troublesome jewellery for some time. But within an hour of Mark Tytherton's tackling his father about it Archie

Tytherton is fishing it out of a drawer in the writing-table in front of us now. The sequence of events is not hard to elucidate. Maurice Tytherton is fond of his son; and he knows perfectly well that he has acted wrongly, and in a fashion justly most offensive to the young man, in doing with his first wife's jewellery as he has done. Hard upon Mark's departure in a passion, therefore, this compunction takes him to Mrs Graves's room, where he demands the jewellery, and receives it. Mrs Graves, is that correct?'

'Yes, that's right. Fair's fair, after all.' Mrs Graves showed no disposition to sulk. 'But what I don't like is the way that young man speaks to me. He ought to take a leaf out of his father's book. Always refined, Mr Maurice Tytherton was.'

'We are gratified to hear it. Very well. Maurice Tytherton receives back the diamonds, returns to this room with them, and for the time being simply puts them away in a drawer. He doesn't know that within a few minutes he will be dead.'

'This woman went straight to Archie, and Archie came straight to this room!' With a sudden and disturbing vehemence, Alice Tytherton had come out with this. 'Everybody knows that, only a few hours before, these two had been in –'

'No doubt. And the fact of Mr Archie Tytherton and Mrs Graves having, shall we say, expressed a passing interest in each other no doubt made Mr Maurice Tytherton the more ready to retrieve the jewellery. So the conjecture Mrs Tytherton has just expressed is at least a tenable one.'

'From which it follows,' Ramsden said, 'that Archie is still by no means out of the wood. He may have to face a good deal more than a mere charge of squalid family pilfering.'

'You keep your mouth shut, you great beast!' It was on

his shrillest note that Archie had produced this. 'I never went near Cynthia. Not again, I mean.'

'Will you allow me to go on?' Appleby looked coldly at both young men. 'I have reached a point within minutes of Maurice Tytherton's being killed. He is sitting in the chair in which his son is sitting now, having thrust the diamonds into that drawer. If you accept – as you will later find I have some reason to do – Archie Tytherton's story, you will see that we are confronted with a very tight time-schedule. Timing, in fact, becomes the crux of the whole matter. So have we much to go on in that regard? For the moment, a good deal less than we could wish. But at least – and very fortunately – Mr Ramsden has a habit of consulting his watch. That gives us one fixed point. For it was at just twenty past eleven that he and Miss Kentwell entered this room and found Maurice Tytherton dead.'

23

'At least we can work some way back from that with a reasonable approximation to accuracy.' Miss Kentwell had abandoned her embroidery and – it might have been felt – a fictitious character with it. 'Mr Ramsden and I had wandered down here from the roof. On the roof we had smoked a cigarette. And we had gained the roof after our first visit to this room, when it was empty. There cannot have been an interval of more than fifteen or twenty minutes between our two visits. And *why* was this room empty on the first occasion? It can only have been because Maurice Tytherton had gone to Mrs Graves's room to recover the diamonds. So not much more than a quarter of an hour has to cover his return with them to this room, his murder, Mr Archie Tytherton's arrival and "rummage" as he calls it, the resulting perfectly revolting theft, and the discovery of the body by Mr Ramsden and myself.'

There was a short silence in the workroom – occasioned, perhaps, by a disposition to make a fresh appraisal of the speaker. When this was broken it was, rather surprisingly, by Catmull.

'Might it be useful to ask, sir, just when the late Mr Tytherton was last seen alive?'

'It certainly might.' Appleby replied to this briskly. 'And the answer appears to be by Mrs Graves, when he visited her and retrieved the diamonds. Mrs Graves, can you put a time to that?'

'Oh yes. It was quite a respectable time for a gentleman to knock on the door. Not late at all. About half-past ten.'

'Madam, are you prepared to swear to that?' This question came from Inspector Henderson, who had hitherto been completely silent. And it came with so professional a snap that Mrs Graves discernibly bounced on the ancient chest upon which she was still sitting. 'It was certainly before eleven o'clock?'

'Yes ... I don't know. I didn't look at *my* watch. But I think so. Just when these things happened can't be important, surely?'

This time, the silence was a baffled one – Henderson's only reply to the lady's question being expressively to compress his lips. And then Carter spoke.

'Those jewels,' he said, 'have made their inglorious exit from the story – and Archie Tytherton with them, I rather suspect. Isn't it time to return to the pictures?' Carter turned arrogantly to Appleby. 'They seem rather to have dropped out of your rambling remarks.'

'I can promise not to do much more rambling.' Appleby was coldly polite. 'It is a matter, is it not, of certain eliminations having to be made? Wouldn't you say, Mr Carter, that it is to the comfort of a number of people that they *should* be made?'

'No doubt.'

'And I am ready to come back to the pictures – including this one.' Appleby had turned round. 'A very fine portrait by Goya, indeed.' He paused. 'But once more, I am afraid, I must move back a little in time. A couple of years, in fact.'

'You be careful, Appleby.' Raffaello, suddenly alerted, had come out with this. 'Anything you say to these people I may take to my solicitor, remember. You'll see.'

'Very well.' Appleby was unimpressed. 'What I am telling these people is that, two years ago, you were knowingly involved in a criminal fraud – and that you are at Elvedon now because you have been in hopes of involvement in another one. If you care to have Inspector Henderson take down these words, I'll sign them on the spot. And you can take them, for all I care, to the entire Law Society. Now, let me get on.'

'Yes,' Mark Tytherton said. 'It's pretty rotten, I expect. But it must come out.'

'I'm afraid it must.' For the first time in his narrative, Appleby hesitated. 'It isn't an aspect of the matter one would want to ventilate, so hard upon your father's death. But here it is – and its background, I believe, is a state of considerable financial stringency at Elvedon. Your father probably inherited rather more in the way of business interests than business ability; there was a good deal in his way of life that cost money; and things just hadn't been going too well. I think it likely that Mr Ramsden could tell us a certain amount about all that.'

'I could,' Ramsden said. 'But the present popular assembly isn't the occasion for it.'

'No doubt you are right. Well, a couple of years ago, Maurice Tytherton, thus embarrassed, was led into a thoroughly fraudulent act.'

'*Led?*' Mark said sharply.

'I should judge so. However, we can't blink the fact of what he did. He caused certain pictures to appear to be stolen; collected money on them from an insurance company; and then quietly sold them through the agency of this disreputable person Raffaello. But this in itself would appear only to have been part of a much larger and more ambitious scheme. It simply released capital for something else. And at this point I think I may introduce to you my colleague Miss Kentwell.'

*

'Sir John expresses the matter most obligingly.' Miss Kentwell was the only member of the company not to be discomposed by Appleby's mild joke. 'I must disclaim any connection, past or present, with the Metropolitan Police.'

'Miss Kentwell works for a private inquiry agency which I have no doubt is of the highest repute. She came to Elvedon – the late Mr Tytherton supposed – entirely in the interest of certain wishes and intentions of his own, which I need not at present particularize. But, in fact, she had a more important client: *Novoexport*.'

'And what the devil,' Carter asked, 'is that?'

'It is the Russian state agency which has the sole control over the export of all works of art from the Soviet Union. As you will know, of recent years the ikonographic art of mediaeval Russia has become extremely popular among collectors, and there has been a great deal of illicit traffic in ikons, whether good, bad, or indifferent. What Maurice Tytherton managed to acquire was a dozen that were very good indeed. With skill, they might be marketed for several times what he gave for them. Only, *Novoexport* – a highly efficient organization – were on his trail.'

'All this,' Carter interrupted, 'has the elements of a capital thriller, no doubt. But I can't see what it has to do with Goya.'

'Just have a little patience, Mr Carter. It is remarkable how things connect up. And now I must mention somebody who requires no introduction to any of you: my friend Mr Catmull.'

'It had nothing to do with me, it hadn't,' Catmull said. His tone mingled truculence and alarm. 'This conspiracy wasn't nothing to me. I didn't accept – and don't none of you think I did – no more than a position of trust, I did.' Under stress of feeling, Catmull seemed to decline into something like the lowly educational status of his wife.

'And very worrying it has been, particularly with that Raffaello – not to speak of Miss Kentwellski – nosing around.'

'Mr Catmull is himself the possessor of a small but choice collection of works of art. They may be viewed – in usefully massive frames – on the walls of his pantry. You will find one of the illicitly acquired ikons behind each. It was an admirably chosen hiding-place – at least of the temporary character required.'

This information, as may be imagined, was variously received by those gathered in the late Maurice Tytherton's workroom. Raffaello produced something between a curse and a groan, and Mrs Graves an uncomprehending stare. Mark Tytherton, who had been reduced to immobility by the record of his father's illegal enterprises, did no more than slightly shake a dazed head.

'But now,' Appleby said, 'let us take a sufficiently broad view of the state of affairs in this house. There has been a pretence of pictures being stolen from it when they haven't been. There has been a hiding away in it of other works of art either stolen or most irregularly come by. There has been the trafficking with Mr Raffaello and, for all I know, others of his kind. It might all be called enough to put funny business with pictures in anybody's head. A little private enterprise, for instance, in the same general territory.' Appleby again turned and glanced at the Goya. 'For example,' he said, 'why not make off with Don Jusepe, or whoever he is, and in some fashion that will result in nobody being much the wiser for quite some time? It's at least an idea, isn't it? And I ought to say it came to Inspector Henderson quite early.'

'Just what came to the Inspector?' Carter asked.

'A notion that made me remember something. And the memory set me to a little investigation this evening.' Appleby put a hand in a jacket pocket. 'In the Elvedon rubbish bins, as a matter of fact. *I cestini dei rifiuti.*' He walked over to a small table, and produced from his pocket and laid upon it half a dozen scraps of multicoloured paper. 'These will do for the moment, although more are available. There happens to be a remarkably good full-size colour reproduction of this Goya – originally the Horton Goya. I know, because I had a copy when little more than a boy. And this small jigsaw will build up into another one. I made a further find in the *cartàccia,* incidentally. But that can keep.'

'How very curious!' Carter had advanced and was studying the scraps of paper thus so strangely brought in evidence. 'Do you mean to say that there was an attempt – apparently an abortive attempt – to substitute *this*' – and he tapped what might have been Don Jusepe's nose – 'for *that*?' His hand had shot out and pointed to the portrait over the fireplace.

'As a matter of fact, I don't.' Appleby spoke very quietly. 'The reproduction was to have no function in this room. It was to have a function, and it *did* have a function, in the identical room directly overhead. Call it the dummy workroom. For this mystery has been very much a matter, you see, of another story.'

Much as if by way of applauding (or, conceivably, censuring) this bizarre joke, a door banged sharply. It was the door of the workroom; Ramsden had vanished through it; and now Henderson was in vain trying to wrench it open again. He had left the key on the other side. And Ramsden had not lacked the presence of mind to turn it in the lock as he departed.

There was a general hubbub. Mrs Graves (who had been behaving very well) had hysterics. Seizing her opportunity, Mrs Tytherton slapped her. Archie Tytherton, exhausted by his perfectly awful day, had fallen to abject blubbering. Raffaello was shouting angrily, as if under the persuasion that some special insult or indignity had been directed upon him. Catmull had picked up a poker, perhaps to beat down the door, or perhaps to defend himself in some imminent lethal affray. Mark Tytherton had leapt to his feet, dashed to the window, and appeared to be measuring the drop to the terrace below. Carter, intending to display detachment and coolness by lighting a cigarette, had actually been sufficiently agitated to burn a finger in the process, and was cursing softly. And the Elvedon peacock chose this propitious moment to scramble to its favourite perch on Hermes and produce a succession of splendid screams.

'Don't jump, Mark,' Appleby said quietly. 'They're keeping a look out below, and he won't get away... Ah! That's better.'

Inspector Henderson had produced a whistle and blown it loudly.

Nevertheless it was a good many minutes before the house guests of the late Maurice Tytherton (together with the attendant Catmull) were released from their confinement. Ramsden had not merely locked them in; he had successfully pocketed the key as he ran. So the door had to be forced open after all – amid a formidable rending of timber – by two burly constables in the corridor. Appleby's patience was untried by all this. He had been in such fracas and confusions before. But he was hardly less upset than Henderson when he was told that the fugitive had vanished.

'But at least he can't have got clean away,' Henderson said. 'Or can he?' He turned to the grim and slightly apprehensive sergeant who was his second-in-command. 'Did anybody hear a car?'

'No, sir. And I don't think he's come downstairs at all. We had the staircases watched.'

'He may have dropped from a window, man. Mr Tytherton here was about to try that ten minutes ago. It could be done.'

'Yes, sir – but where would he be then? The moon's up, and this is a very regular sort of building. These terraces can be commanded by two men – and that's what I've had there.'

'If he hasn't gone down,' Appleby said, 'he has either remained on this floor, or gone up.'

'Quite so, Sir John. It's a matter of one or another of your stories, one may say.' Henderson offered this a shade tartly, but not with positive ill temper. 'The second floor, with your dummy room. Or the third, with all those attics. And he's armed, wouldn't you say?'

'It's certainly very possible that he had on him, or has now picked up, the weapon with which he killed his employer.'

'And he wouldn't stick at killing you or me – or, say, a couple of my men?'

'That I rather doubt. Or not if he has really no chance of getting away. That's my reading of his character, Inspector, for what it is worth. But we're not going to risk the lives of your constables on a hunch like that.' Appleby paused. 'And if it comes to a straight man-hunt, it might go on in those damned attics for days. Do you know what, Henderson? I think I'll take a stroll through them.'

'Well, Sir John, that's more my function than yours, if I may say so.'

'But you may not say so. Or that's how I see the thing.'

'Sir?'

'I'm a retired man, with no standing in this affair at all – except simply as one appealed to, as I think we may call it, by your Chief Constable. But I've held rather a senior job. So will you take an order from me?'

'Yes.'

'Good.' Appleby fleetingly touched Inspector Henderson's arm. 'I'll give your lads a hail,' he said, 'if there's any occasion to call them in.' He hesitated for a moment, and then laughed softly. 'After all, it was my own bloody fault, wasn't it? Showing off like that.'

'Sir?' It would have been fair to describe Henderson as very much shocked.

'I thought, you know, I had another thirty seconds at least. But he saw that he was booked. His mental processes – and his reaction times – are pretty quick.'

'Yes, Sir John. What the old Westerns called quick on the draw. Good luck.'

24

Ramsden was on the roof, and the roof was bathed in moonlight. Near its centre the great lantern which stood poised high above Elvedon's imposing hall cast a shadow like a blunt arrow-head over the gently sloping leaden expanse around it. It seemed an enormous roof: a complication of rising and falling surfaces, of broad plateaus and shallow valleys, of sudden gullies and sharp ridges, all livid and faintly lustrous in the cold illumination now steeping it. Ramsden was perched negligently on a balustrade from which the drop to the south terrace must be sheer. And he had one hand deep in a pocket.

'I'd advise,' he said, 'against coming too near.'

'Thank you, but there's no need. It isn't exactly a death-grapple that's in my mind.'

'You've come to tell me that the game's up, and that I may as well give in?' There was an easy mockery in Ramsden's voice.

'Not really that, either. Almost the reverse, in a way. Haven't you thrown up the sponge rather easily?'

'But *have* I thrown it up? I don't know that I'd noticed.'

'Haven't you bolted in a panic? But perhaps it's been no more than a withdrawal to think things over. Even although you did lock us all in in that childish way. Would you say, Ramsden, that there's really a case against you?'

'Yes, I would. You were just going to embark on it.'

'But a *convincing* case? I'm thinking of a judge and jury.'

'Perhaps that's a different matter.' Ramsden had suddenly turned away. 'May I ask you something, my dear Appleby?'

'By all means. In fact, I undertake to try to answer quite faithfully absolutely any question you care to put to me.'

'What first lodged your sense of the matter quite firmly in your head?'

'Something I was told by your unwitting collaborator, Miss Kentwell. Do you recall trying to prevent her looking out of a window?'

'Ah.'

'I had to ask myself why. You had your wits about you, and knew that there was nothing more alarming or significant in the prospect than a screeching peacock, perched on the head of Hermes. But what about the *viewpoint*? What if it might reveal to her, then or later, that she wasn't where she thought she was? As soon as I'd asked myself that, I saw the truth. The statue of Hermes is directly below Tytherton's workroom, but it is obvious that it is also directly below the room immediately above as well. You and Miss Kentwell were – in the first instance – in that upper room. You didn't want her to see that, on some later occasion in the real workroom, she might become conscious that she was viewing from a perplexingly different elevation. On that, what may be called the whole theory of the dummy room came to me. It was the ingeniously created instrument of an alibi in what was to be a premeditated murder. But juries, you know, don't much care for ingenuity – not, I mean, when it has to be urged by a prosecution. So – seriously – don't you think you still have a chance?'

'Go on, Appleby.'

'The entire architecture of the place favoured the deception. Symmetry, balance, repetition are the key-notes. Grove nods to grove.'

'What's that?'

'Never mind. At least the second floor simply echoes the first. At the same time the scale of the place makes any wandering course through it a bit confusing. Choose somebody – like Miss Kentwell – unfamiliar with the house; conduct her on a rambling tour at night; and she mayn't notice – even though she is a private detective, she mayn't notice! – that the room to which she appears to have been brought back at eleven-twenty is not the room – the absolutely identical room – to which she was introduced at eleven o'clock. And in the interim, during which you haven't been out of her sight, a man appears to have been killed in it. It was as simple as that. But Maurice Tytherton was, in fact, dead in his real workroom before you appeared downstairs and proposed the little tour which took Miss Kentwell into the dummy one.' Appleby paused. 'But consider that jury again. It would want to know how this odd facsimile could be created – and then uncreated.'

'No doubt.' Ramsden had shifted a little on the balustrade, and his hand had gone deeper into his pocket. 'Do tell me all about that.'

'You often had the house virtually to yourself, and on that almost deserted second floor you could go to work at leisure. The workroom isn't copiously furnished, and it was all sufficiently easy, I imagine, to have been quite fun to fudge up. The Goya, as we've seen, was no trouble at all – not for a superficial glance. Nor was a dim old Italian *cassone*. Nor was borrowing, and re-photographing, that photograph of Mark. No, it was all perfectly simple – curtains and rugs and the rest of it – given plenty of time. Of course, dismantling your precious assemblage was another matter. At that, you clearly had to work pretty fast this morning, so that there should be nothing but an innocently empty room again. But among all that endless junk on the floor above, clearly, one could bury a whole houseful of stuff: picture-frame, writing-table, chairs, what you will. It would be quite a job, I imagine, to reassemble that dummy room again now. But I do deprecate your being so casual about the torn-up colour print – to say nothing of the torn-up photograph. That, by the way, was the other scrap of evidence I came upon, with the help of a nice Italian girl, newly arrived in what may be called the family waste-paper basket. You ought to have had your own little bonfire, Ramsden. You really ought.'

'When are you going to tell your friend Henderson all this?'

'Now, now – don't start that lethal rush. Henderson knows it all already. At a pinch, I'd be expendable.'

'And he knows what it was all in aid of?'

'Certainly – and I don't think even that worried jury would lose sleep over that one. You were the master-mind in Elvedon, Ramsden. You ran the place – and perhaps rather more to your own occasional profit than it would have been comfortable for your employer to get to know. But that's speculative, and a minor issue. The bogus robbery two years ago, and the subsequent big *coup* with the profits: you were certainly the controlling intelligence behind both. And when it began to appear that the ikons could produce, even on a black market, a very large sum of money indeed – well, you didn't see why it shouldn't all come to you. There would be only Catmull to square. He had his own plans, perhaps, for double-crossing you. But they would have been ineffectual ones. He's a petty rascal, if ever there was one: of low intelligence, likely to be extremely scared, and ready to make himself scarce at very inconsiderable cost.'

'I wouldn't dispute that character sketch, for what it is worth.' Ramsden laughed softly. 'Of course, a lot of other things were happening at Elvedon. Your jury might find them a shade confusing.'

'Perfectly true. Capable counsel could cast very effective suspicion over at least half a dozen people under this roof now. The unexpected must have come near to unnerving you more than once, Ramsden. Mark's turning up, and proving to have been with his father almost immediately before your own operation was due to begin. The sudden rumpus following Archie's being discovered in bed – if they bothered about a bed – with Mrs Graves. Tytherton's sending for his solicitor. Above all, the shattering realization that Archie had actually been staring at the dead man at an hour which, if it were to be reliably pin-pointed, would blow your whole alibi business sky-high. Yet in all these things there was the positive advantage which might come to you from utter confusion. Your original plan had gone wrong – but you had a chance of getting away with your crime, all the same.'

'Yet I haven't?'

'Let's face it – you have not.' Appleby was suddenly grim. 'The dummy room is a fact. We *can* put it together again, if it takes us a month – and produce sworn testimony that every item was found by the police dispersed through this house. The only two people who could extract an alibi out of it were Miss Kentwell and yourself. And of you two, only you yourself had the time and opportunity to fabricate it. So perhaps, Ramsden, the game *is* up.'

'Yes. Perhaps it is.'

'You had bad luck, I think, in the way your career has fallen out. Maurice Tytherton must have been a pretty poor specimen, it seems to me – although I wouldn't tell Mark so in just those words.'

'Mark knows. But he was rather fond of his father, all the same.'

'It can't be said that you were. You wasted your talents in running Elvedon for him and his rotten crowd. And you resented it.' Appleby paused, and looked sombrely at Ronnie Ramsden. 'But one mustn't get murdering people just because they're rubbishing themselves, and tag around with a pretty grotty set.'

'Thank you, bishop, another sermon.' Ramsden uttered these words mockingly. But he tensed himself as he did so – so that Appleby, who had a developed instinct for danger, found himself doing the same. And Ramsden sensed this. 'All right, all right,' he said. 'I haven't got that gun, as a matter of fact. It's in the lake.'

'Which is not a bad place for it.'

'And what about this place?' Speaking idly now, Ramsden glanced around him, as if suddenly prompted to take the dimensions of Elvedon. 'A ghastly pile' – he tapped lightly with his foot – 'weighed down under all this mass of lead. In this light, it's like an arctic sea. Do you know, Appleby? There's something to be said for being a swimmer into cleanness leaping.'

And suddenly Ramsden was coming at Appleby with a rush. Or so, for only a brief moment, Appleby thought. The lantern was only a little aside from Ramsden's path; he swerved suddenly – to rise as from a spring-board and with perfect timing. There was a crash of glass, and the young man had vanished.

Appleby ran forward, and at the risk of an ugly vertigo stuck his head through the shattered pane. Very far below was the splendid hall of Elvedon, brightly lit. From this viewpoint alone, perhaps, could one be aware of the perfect elegance of its patterned black-and-white marble floor. It was a pattern marred now by a shapeless black splodge in the middle.

Of a fall like that, there could be only one issue. Appleby – as Ronnie Ramsden had claimed to do on another fatal occasion – looked instinctively at his watch. It was just twenty-four hours, he supposed, since Maurice Tytherton had died.

He turned away, left the roof, and descended – rather slowly – through the several stories of Elvedon Court.

LORD MULLION'S SECRET

Mullion Castle nestles in the heart of rural England, the country seat of Lord Mullion.

Charles Honeybath, RA, has been commissioned by Lord Mullion to paint the portrait of Lady Mullion. With his keen eye for facial features and his unerring nose for human motive, Honeybath perceives a peculiar state of affairs at the stately home.

And with Lady Camilla upstairs, old and infirm of mind, holding the key to the family's past and peccadilloes, the chances of discovering the truth are one in a – Mullion.

THE MICHAEL INNES OMNIBUS

Clues baffle and suspects abound in these exhilarating novels: *Death at the President's Lodging, Hamlet, Revenge!* and *The Daffodil Affair*. In them the literary touch of Inspector Appleby is called upon to tackle the macabre murder of a University President, the shooting of the Lord Chancellor while he was acting the part of Polonius, and the simultaneous disappearance of a half-witted girl from London and a half-witted horse from Harrogate.

'A master – he constructs a plot that twists and turns like an electric eel: it gives you shock upon shock and you cannot let go' *The Times Literary Supplement*

Also published

Appleby and Honeybath
An Awkward Lie
The Bloody Wood
Honeybath's Haven
Open House
Seven Suspects

and

The Second Michael Innes Omnibus